DIRTY LITTLE SECRET

DIRTY LITTLE SECRET

THE DEVILS YOU KNOW

SAMANTHA BARRETT

OCTAVIA KNIGHTLY

Are you ready, Little Viper?
Charge that vibrator and enjoy this one handed read
because we all know you'll be tickling that clit after
chapter one.

PLAYLIST

I Wanna Be Yours - Arctic Monkeys
Dirty Little Secret - All-American Rejects
Provider - Sleep Token
Often - The Weeknd
Prisoner - Raphael Lake, Aaron Levy, Daniel Ryan Murphy
Dangerous Woman - Ariana Grande
Swim - Chase Atlantic
Good for You - Selena Gomez, A$AP Rocky
Skin - Rihanna
Straitjackets & Roses - Diggy Graves
Who Do You Want - Ex Habit
Slow Down - Chase Atlantic
Candy - Doja Cat
obsessed - zandros & Limi

Eyes Don't Lie - Isabel LaRosa
My Boy - Billie Eilish
Emo Girl - mgk, WILLOW
LUST - Chase Atlantic
Boyfriend - Dove Cameron
Worship - Ari Abdul
Code Red - Darci
Please - OMIDO & Ex Habit
Slut! (Taylor's Version) (From The Vault) - Taylor Swift
Escapism. - Raye & 070 Shake
The Summoning - Sleep Token

ONE
SAVANNAH

College is a joke!

Scratch that. College *guys* are a joke.

Blake has been acting strange ever since I asked him if we could spice things up a little and maybe try role-playing last weekend. He looked at me like I had grown two heads, then laughed in utter disgust. He told me I watched too much porn, but that's not even half of it. The insults didn't stop there. *Nope.* He told me to get on my knees and suck his dick, and that he would picture someone else. He said that imagining someone else was about as far as he would go in the role-playing department, which isn't even remotely the same thing.

Total fucking jackass, I know.

We got into a huge fight because, of course, I said

no. He didn't even try to understand where I was coming from. He just stormed out of the room like it was on fire, and continued to party with the rest of his frat without me.

Why is shaming women for their sexual desires still a thing?

Have we not evolved?

I thought college would be the place where I found myself. The place where I could experiment with sex before life got too serious. Blake seemed like the perfect guy to do that with. He ticked all the right boxes at the start, though I was so unbelievably wrong about him.

Hindsight's a bitch sometimes.

Now, I'm left with this insatiable need that won't go away because we can't—no, he *won't* satisfy me in the ways that I want him to. *Apparently, eating pussy is beneath the captain of the football team.* Blake's teammates all think he's this amazing guy, and girls literally froth at the mouth when they see him, but they have no idea just how full of shit he really is. Not only is he selfish in the bedroom, but he wouldn't know what respect or consideration was if it bit him in the ass. Much less, where the fucking G-spot is.

Blake is a skilled liar, and I just don't have the energy to put up with him anymore.

I'm done.

I've sent him a dozen text messages and tried to call to meet up, hoping to end things. He may be a jackass, but I'm not, and if I'm going to break up with somebody, they at the very least deserve a conversation and to be told in person.

Blake, however, is ghosting me, making this whole thing drag out longer than it needs to, and I just want to cut all ties and move on.

Fucking coward.

To make matters worse, my stepbrothers are in Blake's fraternity, and they hate him with a passion. They've been hounding me to break up with him for months now, and the last thing I want to hear is their inevitable *'I told you so, Savannah'* spiel that will undoubtedly follow when they learn that I finally listened to them. Well, they aren't the reason behind why I'm breaking up with him. I couldn't care less what my stepbrothers think about who I am dating. Still, something about them knowing what's good for me sets me on edge in ways I'm not sure I even want to unpack.

Kale and Reign Jagger are fucking hot.

I'm talking weak in the knees, bedroom eyes,

panty-dropping kind of hot. I know, I know, I shouldn't be looking at them in that way, but name a single woman on campus who wouldn't, and I'll stop. They are the embodiment of every dark and depraved fantasy I swore I'd outgrow, but can't seem to quit. Tattooed, muscular bodies, jawlines that could cut glass, not to mention, they have abs for fucking days. Add in the fact that they are twins, and you have yourself a walking orgasm.

It's so completely wrong in all the ways that have always felt so right to me in my mind. No matter how many times I try to ignore the way my heart flutters whenever they're near me, or try to convince myself that it's nothing more than curiosity. A childhood crush I've developed because they're so close to me, yet so untouchable. I can't seem to stop.

Are they the reason every other man feels wrong? Has my mind grown so consumed by them that all the guys I date are nothing more than inconsequential side characters and don't even remotely come close to those two?

And at times when I think I've got everything under control, they go ahead and do something subtle that makes me question whether or not I'm alone in feeling these hidden desires.

The tilt at the corner of their full lips when they

catch me staring, their fingers brushing against mine as we walk past each other in our hallway when it was unnecessary.

I've told myself that I'm only seeing what I want to see—subscribing to the delusion that only I have created. Still, I can't help but sense that Kale and Reign know exactly what they're doing to me. I can't bring myself to feel ashamed about it, and I don't want them to stop.

Their best friend, Jackson Graves, is just as fucking good-looking and it kills me when I see the three of them together, shirtless and working out in the gym, or hanging out by the pool at our parents house. The images I conjure in those moments are enough to get me on a one-way ticket to hell, but I don't care. Not in the slightest. It's not like they will ever know that I dream about the three of them using me and taking whatever the fuck they want while wringing out orgasm after orgasm from me.

Dear Lord, please forgive me for envisioning fucking my stepbrothers and their best friend.

TWO
REIGN

She thinks we have no idea that she wants to end things with that pipe smoker, Blake. It's clear as fuck to anyone with a set of eyes whenever they're together that he's not good enough for her, and deep down, she knows it.

Savannah Carter is fine wine and silk. Blake Humphries is trailer trash in a jersey, and the human version of the warm side of a pillow. He's never treated our little Savy right, and I'm surprised she even gave him the time of day to begin with.

They are polar opposites.

Where Blake is a preppy, prudish, bastard jock, she's a fucking viper. *Hypnotizing.* She draws you in with just a glance, and before you know it, you're on your knees like some lovesick fool, addicted to her poison. There's no mistaking that Savy is a total freak in the sheets. She has that way about her. Everything she does is one hundred percent seductress and sin, and it's obvious that she's holding back because of that douche.

It's criminal.

She deserves to feel satisfied in all the right ways, and the sooner she kicks that asshole to the curb, the better. That way, Kale, Jackson, and I can finally make our move.

"Have you noticed he's avoiding her?" Kale says from beside me. I look up to see Blake rushing in the other direction, and Savy just standing there, one hand on her hip, the other clenched tight at her side as she stares after him, a look of annoyance and disgust plastered across her beautiful face. Her body is to die for. She has curves in all the right places, and that asshole Blake sure as fuck doesn't appreciate her enough.

"Check this out." Both Kale and I tear our gaze from her to see Jackson holding a flyer. I roll my eyes at the fucking thing.

"I'm not going to a fucking Halloween party," I bite out.

Jax narrows his green eyes at me. "It's a party in

the fucking woods, you dumbass, and judging by the look of things, she's single now."

"You think?" Kale says, as if the thought is too good to be true, no matter how inescapable their break-up is. I look over to see that Savannah has stormed off, and the corner of my lips tilts into a smile.

"Trouble in paradise?" I say with a smug grin, and I don't bother hiding the thrill in my voice.

"Isn't it obvious? Anyway, you fucking idiots, everyone will be in costumes, which means that this is the perfect opportunity for us to wear masks and chase her ass down. She will never know that it's us. The thought of finally fucking her senseless and making her embrace that depraved little demon inside her has me growing all kinds of hard," Jax says, and Kale shoots him a knowing look. My cock twitches in my jeans at the thought of Jackson being hard with our Little Viper on her knees, begging for a sweet fucking taste.

"She won't know what hit her," my twin says, and I nod because it's true.

Savannah has always belonged to us, whether she wants to admit it to herself or not, and the sooner she accepts it, the sooner she can stop denying what she truly craves.

To be fucked by my twin brother, my best friend, and me.

I still remember the summer we went back home, and she walked in on Kale and me fucking Jackson. The look on her face was priceless, and the fact that she didn't run away shrieking was all I needed to know.

She wanted us, too.

She has practically salivated over us for years now, curious to get a little taste of what my boys and I have to offer. Knowing that she couldn't tear her eyes from mine while I came all over Jackson's mouth that day makes wanting her that much more addictive. She hasn't uttered a single word to anyone about it, trust me, I'd know if she had. Because what she saw... let's just say that we weren't *gentle*.

That's just how we like it.

We've all fucked girls before. Individually, and all together. I've lost count of how many. But none of those women ever understood the dynamic between the three of us.

But our dirty Little Viper does.

Without a word, she simply stood there. Her wide, grey-blue eyes glazed over with desire and need, lost to a lust-fueled trance. She was captivated by the devilish things her stepbrothers were getting up to with their best friend, and our little Savy wanted in.

"Do you think she'll be there?" Kale asks, and I can tell that his thoughts are racing a mile a minute.

"Of course she'll fucking be there. Besides, we can just force her to go if she shows signs of bailing, though something tells me she won't say no," I say before standing, my eyes involuntarily searching the spot where Savy disappeared. Kale has wanted Savannah for as long as Jackson and I have, and as desperately. And when Halloween comes, that desperate need will finally ignite into a dark, uncontrollable blaze, impossible to tame.

We'll watch the heat spill from her like blood until she's begging—no, *screaming* for us to fuck her. We'll feed off every fragment of her surrender, lose ourselves in her chaos until she comes so completely undone, she won't ever dream of someone else touching her.

God help the motherfucker who dares to try because I'll put them so deep in the fucking earth they'll be sprouting roots.

She's ours.

Always was, and always will be.

And once we claim what's ours, there's no turning back.

THREE
SAVANNAH

I didn't want to come to this party, but this is the only place that Blake can't avoid me. He still hasn't responded to my calls or messages, but tonight, I am ending things with him, party be damned. Music blares through the speakers, some song about wanting to be someone's vacuum cleaner bouncing off the walls, and I search the familiar crowd for signs of Blake or his teammates. Everyone is dressed in some elaborate costume, and the dark, smoky lighting gleaming through the fog machines makes it hard to recognize who is who. The smell of sweat, cheap beer, and dollar-store cologne hangs in the air as I push through the drunken bodies grinding against each other.

I skipped last year's party, deciding I'd much

rather spend Halloween watching horror movies alone in my dorm room with my good, old faithful vibrator, instead of partying with a bunch of college students dressed up as slutty vampires.

There's nothing like a man wearing a ghost mask, chasing you with a knife to get you going, am I right?

Or maybe that's just me.

From what I can already tell, I would have been better off doing the same thing again this year.

"Yessss, bitch! You came!" A drunken, high-pitched voice cuts through the music, and I turn my head just in time to catch my best friend, River, throwing her arms around me. I stagger back a little, my own arms wrapping around her just in time to stop us from collapsing to the floor. This woman is absolutely feral, but I love her for it.

"Hey, Boo Boo." I laugh, holding her steady. River's vampire fangs are crooked in her mouth, and her fake blood is now smeared across both of us.

"First of all, what the hell have you come as?" she asks, her perfectly tweezed brows rising in approval, examining me from head to toe. I didn't have much to work with, so I settled on the only thing I could find in my closet that looked halfway decent.

"Vampire slayer," I supply as she turns to face

someone, and pries what looks to be two freshly poured beers in red solo cups from his hands.

"Thanks, Connor," River says, batting her lashes at the poor guy dressed as Superman, who smiles down at her like she hung the moon.

That's my bestie, ladies and gentlemen.

We've been best friends for as long as I can remember, and she knows me better than I know myself. She's the only one who knows about my *secret,* and believe it or not, River has been the one begging for me to pursue something with them, all three of them, since high school.

My eyes scan the party, still searching for Blake, when something catches my eye in my periphery. I turn to see him, hidden within decorative cobwebs in the corner, sucking face with Molly fucking Akers. His hands are on her waist, pinning her against his body, her arm is wrapped around his neck, her free hand in his hair, and I wait for the anger to come, but it doesn't. I don't feel anything but sheer annoyance at myself for even wasting my time with that fucking prick.

I take a step forward, then another. I'm not sure what I even plan to do at this moment, but before I can decide, the music stops. The lights go out, and we're shrouded in darkness. A voice comes up behind me, River's voice, and she links her arm with mine, pulling me away.

"It's party time, babe."

Wait, this wasn't the party?

River weaves through the crowd, her arm still tangled in mine as everyone makes their way toward the back exit.

"Where are we going?" I ask as we cross the backyard and into the woods behind the frat house. Everything is dark, save for the neon glow of the moonlight, and it's obvious that I didn't get the memo that we'd be taking the party elsewhere. If I had, I probably wouldn't have come at all. River just laughs, tugging me along as we tread through the thicket of trees with the rest of the party-goers.

"The real party is in the woods, Savannah! That's where all the fun is," she says, garnering a few cheers from nearby drunken listeners.

I have to admit, it's giving *Halloween vibes*, so I guess partying in the dark makes sense. I reach into my pocket for my phone with my free hand and shoot off a text to Blake, because at this point, that's the only goodbye he deserves.

Savannah:

It's over, asshole. Lose my number.

I don't bother waiting for a reply, knowing he's otherwise *occupied*, and switch my phone off.

Fuck him.

Leaves crunch beneath my Doc Martins, and I'm grateful for my leather jacket as the temperature drops the further into the woods we go.

"Aren't you cold?" I look over at River's exposed shoulders, almost gleaming in the dark.

"Haven't you heard, thot's don't get cold, babe," she replies through a chuckle.

"You're incorrigible."

The deep rumble of motorcycles echoes through the trees, and River shoots me a glance, the shadows doing fuck all to hide her knowing expression. A wave of nervous anticipation ripples over me, before a familiar heat settles low in my stomach.

I know who they belong to.

By the time we reach the lake, a bonfire is already blazing. Music pulses around us, and people are already hooking up, seemingly unaware or maybe just uncaring of their audience.

I want that!

I never had anything like that before, and PDA was never Blake's thing. At least, it wasn't when he was with me. He wouldn't even hold my hand or hold me whenever his friends were around.

Fuck that guy and his pencil dick. I guess he's Molly Akers' problem now.

All I ever wanted was to feel desired, and not like I was a fucking side-piece.

I am the main event. Period.

Don't get me wrong, I don't want to be owned or anything, but I'd like everyone to know that I have a man. And for my man to stake his claim so no other fucker tries to come at me with the hope of getting a sliver of my attention.

I want to be chased and dominated.

I want to submit to a man's control, but only because I know that he will keep me safe. I want someone I can trust, who will never hurt me, and for everyone to know that I am the most important thing in his whole fucking life.

But tonight? I want to be the fire that sparks through his veins until he's addicted to the burn.

Whoever he is.

Even if they'll never be who I truly want.

FOUR

KALE

Jackson stands at my side while Reign leans against a nearby tree, surveilling the party. From the minute we showed up, we had every girl's attention on us, as usual. Whenever their polo-wearing ass boyfriends aren't around to watch them get fucked, they circle the three of us like vultures, fiending for a taste of the bad boys. Then they run along, back to their boyfriends, playing the doting girlfriend with hearts in their eyes.

As much as I don't blame them for their attraction to us, it isn't the attention of these bitches that we want. There is only *one* girl we came here for, and she's currently standing by the edge of the bonfire looking hot as fuck beside her best friend.

River Morgan is good people, and we like her

because she isn't a thirsty fucking bitch like everyone else around here. She looks out for Savannah, and that means something to us.

One night, while at our parents' house for the holidays, we overheard them having one of those girly, *deep and meaningful conversations.*

It wasn't like we meant to eavesdrop, River is just a little on the clamorous side, making it way too fucking easy for us to listen.

When she told Savannah not to hold back where we're concerned, at first, we were all a little stunned. Not stunned that Savannah had a thing for us, that was so fucking obvious. We were shocked that River didn't care that we were her best friend's stepbrothers, which was the only reason we've held back from claiming our girl all these years.

While Savannah might have had it bad for us, Jax included, this thing we feel for her is beyond some *little crush.* She's the sky wrapped in starlight, designed to be worshipped.

Mine.

Ours.

And we'll make her see galaxies she never fucking knew existed.

Yes, we're all wearing masks tonight, and there's a chance she won't know it's us when we finally take what's ours, but we'll make sure we ruin her for any other motherfucker either way. Because the truth is, we were made for each other, and I know that she knows it, too.

"It's time," I announce to the guys as Savannah turns away from the fire and starts walking into the woods.

Silly girl.

She has no idea that she's about to be hunted and owned by us in mere minutes, and I can't fucking wait to finally claim what's always been mine.

Both Reign and Jax swing their gazes to me and nod. "Let's go get our girl," Reign growls, and I don't miss the hunger swirling around his gravelly tone.

"Fuck, I'm already hard," Jax says, garnering a chuckle from Reign and me. He's always had a flair for the dramatics, but of the three of us, Jax is the most submissive one. He relinquishes his control to please us in the bedroom, though I have a feeling things might be a little different when we finally capture our girl.

There's a darkness circling within his green irises that says the submissive side we've come to know and love has left the building, and there's no denying that I like it.

We stick to the shadows, setting off after her as

she vanishes further into the woods, completely unaware of the predators lingering in the darkness, ready to devour her. The three of us spread out. Trapping her will be much easier if she's cornered with nowhere to run. I take the middle while Reign and Jackson take to the sides, and with each calculated step, I can feel the adrenaline pumping through my veins like a hit of cocaine, and I already know that with just one taste of her, I'll be addicted.

The moonlight shines through the swaying branches, making it easier for me to see, and when my gaze lands on Savannah, her long white hair gleaming in the dark, everything stops.

I keep my breathing slow, my steps quiet and steady. As I close in on her, anticipation pulls me closer to where she is. We have waited long enough for this night, and not even death could hold us back now.

Savannah's arms are wrapped around her middle, and every sound she hears has her all jumpy and tense. She's on edge and scared out of her fucking mind, though she knew that she would be and walked into the woods anyway. She's the only girl I've ever met who loves fear. Little does she know, we're all just as bad as she is.

I focus on her, whipping her head in every direction, as she attempts to make sense of her surroundings.

She knows that she's being watched. She can feel our eyes on her. Yet, our bodies are wrapped in darkness, and she can't see a fucking thing. I want her out of her mind with fear because I know she wants that shit, and I sure as fuck won't be the one to deny her.

Savannah stops dead in her tracks and slowly turns, looking for whoever is following close behind. I give her points for instinct, though there's very little she can do to stop what we have planned for her. I duck behind a tree and use it for cover. She can't see me. I know she can't because she looks in every other direction except where I'm hiding. Me, on the other hand, I can see her clear as day, well... *almost*, and fuck if my mouth isn't watering for a taste of that sweet pussy I've been dreaming about for years.

"Who's there?" she calls out. But of course, her question is met with silence. Savannah isn't at all stupid. She knows she isn't alone in these woods. "I swear to God I will kick your ass—"

Her threat is cut off when I step out from behind the tree. Her eyes widen at the sight of me, and she stumbles back a step.

"God can't save you from the devils that hunt you, baby."

Her jaw unhinges, and her shadowed face pales. "W-what do you want?"

"To see inside you," Jackson answers, his large frame stepping into the moonlight from the shadows on her left. She whirls around and it almost costs her, because she stumbles, nearly falling over. Savannah looks between the two of us, her mind racing as she tries to figure out a way to escape. I audibly chuckle, and her head flicks back to me.

There is no exit for her.

This is happening, and she needs to accept that because I'm not letting her go. Tonight, I'm going to live out every fantasy I have ever fucking had about her and force her to crave me as much as we crave her.

"Who the fuck are you?" she shouts, letting her fear rise to the surface.

"The devils you know," Reign says from behind her. This time when she turns around, she loses her footing, falling flat on her ass. Savannah stares up at him with a fear-filled expression, then starts crab-crawling backwards. She doesn't make it far before she collides with Jackson's legs, and the scream that escapes her now trembling lips is divine. She moves as fast as she can away from him.

"Get the fuck away from me!" she snarls, her wide eyes glimmering with unshed tears.

"It's cute that you think you're the one in charge here, barking out orders like that. But you're not, baby girl. We are," I growl, my eyes raking over her petite frame, only stopping when I reach her wild, beautiful eyes.

"We're going to give you ten seconds to leave," Jackson says, and her eyes widen with panic.

"Ten, nine, eight..." She doesn't move as Jackson starts counting down, and a mix of confusion and trepidation forms on her moonlit face. Her eyes bounce between each of us, contemplating her options, but it's too late for her.

"Three, two, one... *Run.*"

"Ready or not, Little Viper," Reign taunts, taking a step closer to her.

"We're coming for you," I almost chant the words, and in the next breath, she pushes to her feet, taking off through the woods. The three of us run after her without a word, overtaken by the thrill of the chase and the inherent need to capture and claim her. She can lie to herself all she likes and say she doesn't want this, but she can't lie to us. I've read her journal. I know this is one of her fantasies, and she is going to love every fucking second of it. She's going to enjoy every goddamn fucking inch of us buried deep in all her holes.

Savannah rounds a large bend and makes the mistake of peering back over her shoulder to see how far behind we are. It costs her precious time, jeopardizing her lead, and Jackson uses her error to his advantage. He pushes his legs harder, then leaps into the air, tackling her to the ground. I hear all of the air rush out of her lungs, and she tries to fight him off, but it's futile. Jax easily overpowers her, forcing her to submit to him like a *good girl*.

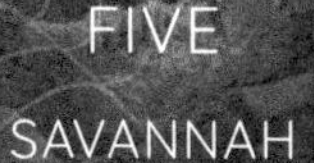

The pressure of his body pressed against mine has rendered me completely immobile.

I'm at his mercy, *their mercy,* and there's not a single thing I can do about it.

The masked stranger grips my wrists and pins them above my head, tangling them in my hair, then throws his leg over me, straddling my waist. A whimper escapes me when I can feel his hard cock pressed against my heated core, then I look up and come face to face with a mask worthy of a horror film. The skull looks depraved, sinful even, sending a trickle of ice down my spine. His two accomplices wear the same masks and flank him on either side. There is something so sinister about the way they're watching me, and the fear coursing through me only adds to my heightened arousal.

I shouldn't be feeling this way, so okay with being scared, but I can't help it. My pussy is pulsing, and my panties are damper than they've ever been in my life. This is the moment I've spent years dreaming of—the highlight of my every secret fantasy.

There's only one detail missing.

"Look at you, Little Viper. Your mouth says you don't want this, but I bet that pretty little cunt of yours is dripping, *trembling* for us to touch it." I bite the inside of my cheek to keep from whimpering. If he presses his cock any harder against my body, he'll be able to feel just how much I *do* want this.

"Who the fuck are you?" I force as much resent-ment into my tone as I can, but even I can hear how unconvincing I am. Thank God I chose Fine Arts as my major and not Performing Arts. I'd have flunked out in the first year.

"I already told you. We are the devils you know, baby," the guy on the right says, his voice filled with a mix of longing and greed, and the knowledge that the three of them want me like this has me throwing caution to the fucking wind.

Blake never wanted to do anything like this,

despite putting myself out there and asking, and I'll be fucking damned if I let this opportunity slip through my fingers. This might be the last time anything like this ever happens to me, and it's that thought that has me wanting so desperately to embrace this moment with them.

I don't care if this is wrong.

"What are you going to do with me?" My voice is thick and full of wanton lust, and I focus my eyes, trying to see as much of them as I can in the dark. They're tall and broad, that much I can tell, and it only makes me want to do this again in the daylight.

"Anything we fucking want," the guy on the left says, his voice is low and hoarse, and I could have sworn that I've heard it before. The guy straddling me skates his one hand up my body without an ounce of hesitation, and it sends a rush of heat all over me.

His movements are sure and precise as he grabs my tit, squeezing it hard, drawing a loud moan from me. I'm not even embarrassed by my reaction to his touch. If they wanna fucking play, I'll give them a game worth playing.

"You want us to take what we want from you, Little Viper?" he asks, using the same nickname the other guy did before. When I don't respond, he pinches my nipple between his fingers, causing me to gasp. My body lifts up into him, and I've never craved anyone like this before.

I can feel him everywhere, and all sense of logic flies right out the window when our eyes meet.

Who is this man?

As much as I think I'd like to know, there's something about being alone in the dark with three masked strangers that I find so damn alluring.

I'm drowning in desire.

Need and uncontrollable want are pulling me under, and I have never felt more alive.

"I want you to use me," I finally say, and I can feel their eyes on me, waiting for me to give them more. I'm aware they're hanging onto my every word, hoping that I'd submit to them. "I want you to make me fucking beg," I rasp, my throat thick with the need to cry out at how good the man's hard body feels grinding against mine, enough to leave me breathless, and craving more.

So much more.

The other guys standing in the dark above me let out a groan as they wait on the sidelines, watching their friend rock against my needy pussy beneath the light of the moon.

"You fucking like that? You like watching him

claim what's yours? *Are you jealous you won't ever get a turn?"* I taunt. My lips tilt into a smirk, and it's all I can do not to laugh when they snarl, dipping their heads to the side like the predators that they are. Their large, muscular bodies grow rigid in the darkness, as the air around me morphs into something cold and menacing. I imagine their tight jaws clenching behind their masks as they battle with their composure, losing patience with me.

I doubt they expected that I would be this way. I wonder if they knew that of all the women who could be in my place, I'd be the one who craves the chase. Craves the hunt. Something is telling me that I'm on dangerous ground, though. Toying with their barely there control, that's hanging on by a thread like it's nothing more than a light switch.

Fire playing with an even bigger fire.

I hope they know what they are getting themselves into because the flames don't fucking scare me, not even a little. The coldness that follows does, and I refuse to let this go without first feeling everything they want to make me feel. So if they're as ready as they seem to be, I will gladly hand them the match, and we can all burn together.

SIX

JACKSON

I grind my cock against her pussy, her tight leggings doing little to hide her reaction to me. The moan that tumbles from her full lips has me growing even harder, and I can't hold back any longer. I need to taste her, *feel* her wrapped around my cock. When I finally have her pussy dripping for me as I slam inside, taking whatever the fuck I want from her, I might just come undone.

We're going to push her limits, because we all know that's what she wants. We'll force our way inside her until she's seeing stars. She'll have no idea where the fuck she begins and we end, and our Little Viper won't ever want to give us up.

"We're going to own every inch of you," I snarl, her leather jacket long gone as I grip the middle of her shirt, tearing it open with little effort, exposing her lacey black bra.

She's trying to kill me.

I pull the cups down, exposing her full, beautiful tits, her nipples hardening from the cool night air and arousal—my mouth waters with the need to taste them.

I'm starving for her.

Knowing I can't remove the mask, I push to my feet and loom above her. Reign and Kale are on either side of me, and I feel at home like this. With them by my side, and our girl powerless before us, there's nothing I could ever want more. "Head down, ass up," I demand, my voice leaving no room for protest. Her eyes glaze over, swimming with lust and submission as she obeys me without a single complaint. I knew she wouldn't. I knew she'd be our perfect girl.

Kale crouches down, his large shadow shrouding her delicate frame from the light, as he shreds her black leggings from her body with his bare hands. Savannah gasps, her wide eyes furious at the act, and I can't say that I blame her. At the rate we are destroying her clothing, she will be limping out of here in nothing but her thong and bra. The idea of her walking around like that has my cock jerking in my jeans, and I want nothing more than for our girl to wear proof that all three of us have claimed her. I don't give a single fuck who sees.

Savannah Carter is ours.

"*Fuck*, that ass is just begging for my cock, isn't it, Little Viper?" Reign grits out, and I can tell his restraint is starting to wear thin.

He wants her, and he wants her now.

Get in fucking line, lover.

"Her mouth is mine," Kale adds, yet before either of them can make a move, I take control. "None of you are touching her until I taste that perfect little cunt. I want her shaking and screaming before anyone's cocks go anywhere near her holes. Am I fucking clear?" I can feel each of their gazes on me, no doubt shocked by my dominant tone.

I don't ever use it with them.

That's just not how we are together. Yet, the heat rolling off them tells me they like it. Maybe a little too much. I keep my focus on Savannah, relishing in the fact that I hold all the power here. Usually, the twins take control, and it's always like that when we fuck. I submit to them willingly and gladly, but that's not happening with her. I crave—*no*, I need to be in control.

I drop to my knees behind her now exposed,

round ass, and push her thong to the side, revealing her bare, pretty pink pussy, glistening with proof that we were right about her. Almost in sync, the three of us groan at the sight of her arousal coating her inner thighs, and fuck if I don't get to lick it up, knowing we're the reason that it's there.

"Keep your fucking head down or I'll stop eating *my* pussy, got it?" I command.

"Y-yes," she stutters, and I push my mask up, resting it on top of my head, and lean forward, inhaling her heady scent. *Fuck,* the smell of her alone has me wanting to bust a nut.

"Fuck this, get that ass up now, I'm fucking you while you eat that filthy little slut's cunt," Reign barks impatiently, not used to me being the one throwing around orders. My dick is so fucking hard right now at the thought of having him inside me while I taste her.

Doing as he says, I shift onto my hands and knees, then bury my face into her. The instant her sweet taste hits my tongue, I growl in satisfaction.

For years, I have wondered what she would taste like, salivated over the thought of having the twins and her at the same time, but nothing I have conjured in my mind compares to the taste that I'm experiencing right now.

She's so fucking hot, and I am addicted.

Reign reaches around and unbuckles my jeans, pulling them down over my hips. "Shit, man, can I fuck her mouth, *please?*" Hearing Kale ask me for permission draws a deep groan from me, and I pull back to look over my shoulder at him.

"Make her take every inch of that cock, baby," I answer. A noticeable shudder rolls over my best friend as he nods, moving to the front of our girl, positioning himself on his knees before her mouth.

I swipe my tongue from asshole to clit, and I love how she trembles. Savannah is so responsive, and when she pushes back against my tongue and begins grinding her pussy against it, I lose all train of thought until I feel Reign ease inside me.

I purr into her pussy at the feeling of him slowly filling my ass, and when he grabs my waist roughly and moans into the night air, I smirk, still tasting her wet cunt. He knows I love to be fucked hard and rough, and he does it so fucking well.

When the sounds of our Little Viper slurping Kale's girth fill our ears, both Reign and I weaken. I can just picture her choking on his thick dick, spit dripping down her chin. I want to taste them like that, and I make a mental note for next time.

"Swallow my big fucking dick, baby," Kale

praises, and her pussy throbs, pulsing against my tongue.

She likes to be praised. She and Kale have that in common.

"Fuck!" I grit out when Reign slams his hard length all the way inside me, stretching my tight hole so fucking good that I almost black out from the sheer ecstasy.

"Take my cock, motherfucker, you know you want it," he pants through clenched teeth. He fucks into me hard and fast, making Savannah moan as his thrusts push my tongue deep into her cunt, her mouth stuffed with an almost delirious Kale.

I suck her clit into my mouth as I press back against Reign, urging him to fuck me harder. His thrusts grow wild, pounding into me like a man starved, and his large, rough hands grip my hips as he drives into me with reckless abandon, chasing his release.

I want him to ruin me. I want them to use me, and our girl, until there's nothing fucking left. Instead, the fucker stops, pulling out of me slowly, and I ignore the irritation that always follows when he doesn't finish me like this.

Leaves crunch beneath his booted feet as he walks around to stand beside Kale. And it's too dark for me to determine what exchange passes between them. Silently, Kale walks behind me. His cock, a little bigger than his brother's, pushes against my hole, and the irritation I felt before is long gone, replaced with excitement. Our Little Viper has worked him into a frenzy, which means he won't hold back with me.

"Open your dirty mouth," Reign says, looking down at our girl, and I look up to watch as his hips move forward, her lips wrapping so nicely around his cock, that five seconds ago was fucking my ass senseless.

My own cock is hard as a fucking rock at the sight, and when Kale pushes the back of my head down into her pussy again, he doesn't remove his hand. He holds me there. My nose brushes against her sweet hole, my lips sucking on her, and when I feel him stretch me, all fucking bets are off.

He drives his cock into me in one hard thrust, until he is buried so deep inside that I stop fucking breathing. I don't even realize that my mouth is no longer on Savannah's pussy, until Kale fists my hair, pulling my head backward so that I can look up at him. His face is obscured, but I know he needs to look into my eyes when we're like this. He needs connection in ways Reign doesn't, and every time we fuck, we get closer and closer to each other. If that's even possible.

"Did I fucking say that you could stop?" Reign barks, his jaw tight as he fucks our girl's throat, and we know he isn't talking to her. Kale releases his hold on my hair and looks over at Reign.

"What's the matter, you jealous that I'm fucking our guy while your cock is buried deep inside our girl's mouth?" Kale taunts, and I love it when they get greedy because the angrier they are, the harder they fuck, and at this point, if I don't fucking come in the next few minutes, I'll die.

I'm so fucking gone for them.

Reign pulls out of Savannah's mouth, before he slowly kneels, getting to her level.

"Do you like being used like this, baby?" he soothes, raising his hand to brush away the white strands of hair sticking to her face from saliva, pre-cum, and sweat.

"Y-yes," she says, her voice all breathy and exhausted, and it must do something to Kale, because he stops thrusting and pulls out of me, walking to stand beside his twin.

Oh, this should be fun.

I waste no time standing, adjusting my mask until

it's back in place, and moving to stand on the other side of Reign as the three of us gaze down at her. She looks totally fucked, yet none of us have had her yet.

"Do you want to taste what you do to us, Little Viper?" Reign questions, and the desire in his voice almost makes me whimper. Savannah looks up at us and nods in answer.

"I wanna hear you fucking say it," Reign demands, and even though we're in the dark, I don't miss the twitch in her upper lip.

She's hiding a smile, which tells me that our woman likes this a little more than I thought she would. Clearing her thoroughly fucked throat, her slumped shoulders straighten, and all three of us go still.

"I want you all at the same time. I want to watch as you drain your cocks of cum from fucking your fists while you stare down at my bare tits. I want you to mark me, claim me, then once I am covered in your cum, I want all three of you to lick me fucking clean."

Holy fucking shit.

I think I just died and, for some miraculous fucking reason, I've wound up in heaven.

Little Savannah Carter not only has a dirty

mouth on her, but she's also dark, depraved, and filthy as all hell.

We had her all figured out the moment we laid eyes on her. She walked into her new stepbrother's home, all doe-eyed and *innocent* in a tight little skirt. Yet, she didn't even come close to fooling us. We knew there was a demon hidden somewhere deep inside her, and it has finally come out to play.

"Is that right, baby girl?" Kale says, and I can tell in his voice that he's beaming. There is a hint of newfound admiration for his secret obsession, and I've got to say, I'm right there with him.

"Yes. I want it. I want all of it. With you," she replies, staring up at us all starry-eyed, our masks not hiding our lust-drunk condition. Part of me wants to tear the fucking mask completely off and let her know it's me that she's claiming, but I don't.

Instead, I take back my control and move away from Reign's right to stand in between the twins, wishing I could see the look on their faces. I wait before our girl, and it's a sight I could die looking at. The moon is higher in the sky now, and she looks fucking luminous.

An angel, I tell myself, as she reaches out to cup my heavy balls, then takes my cock in her mouth without another word. The world around me stills as she takes all of me in, slurping and sucking up my pre-cum, put there by being edged all night.

Little does she know that she's been edging me for a lot longer than that.

When my tip hits the back of her throat, her hands reach up, cupping my ass, pulling me further into her mouth.

No gag reflex? *This woman.*

I need to touch something.

I reach for my guys, gripping their cocks in each hand as they stand taut beside me, watching Savannah eat me up like this will be the last time we will ever see her like this.

It won't be.

Over my dead fucking body is she walking away from us now. Not when I know how sweet her pretty cunt tastes.

I work my fists over their cocks, stroking them until they buck into my palms, wrapped tightly around them. My chest is heaving, my breaths are uneven as Kale's head tips back, giving in to the sensation that's pulling all of us closer to the edge. My balls tighten, throbbing with the need to come when Savannah's tongue circles my swollen tip, then moves down to lick my balls, wet with her saliva.

I look over at Reign, his fingers sliding gently into

her hair, and he grips my left shoulder with the other, steadying himself, feverish from the hand fuck I'm giving him.

"God, you feel so fucking good, baby," he breathes, and our girl mewls at the sweet words he says only to me. "*Fuck, b-baby...*" he rasps, all signs of the tough guy completely thrown to the fucking wayside, and I know that he's almost there.

I hold off on my own orgasm just to burn this moment into my memory, because this is the hottest thing I've ever done in my life.

"Yeah, you like that, love? You like it when I beat your cock into oblivion?" I rasp, almost breathless as I work them both frantically.

"Your hand is fucking magic, babe." This comes from Kale, looking all sorts of intoxicated as his cock begs for release. "Our girl is doing such a good fucking job pleasing you, isn't she?" he says before groaning, jolting hard into my palm. He reaches out, gripping hold of my other shoulder, just like his brother is on my other side, and when we look down at our girl, that's all it fucking takes.

"Oh God. I'm coming!" Kale cries out, unravelling with each pump of my fist.

"Are you coming for me?"

"Y-yes, I'm coming for you."

Kale is fucking sobbing right now.

Savannah leans back, releasing my cock, her tits glowing in the moonlight as Kale bucks once. Twice. Three times before hot spurts of cum erupts from his pulsating dick, coating her collarbone and chest.

Reign isn't far behind him as he rocks into my palm. He hauls me closer, reaching down to grip me, and he wastes no time fucking my hard cock with his rough hand in front of her face.

His hips don't stop moving, as we find our rhythm, our eyes not leaving the beauty before us, painted with my best friend's release.

"Come with me."

"I'm coming, lover," I whisper back, and we both let out a low, breathy whine as our bodies shudder against each other. "Fuck... *ah*, yes, baby," I moan, my voice ragged, before we're both coming apart at the seams.

Savannah holds out her tongue this time, and I know that it's because she desperately wants to taste us, whatever way she can.

Our hot cum spills out, coating her tongue and chin, as well as her glistening breasts, bouncing as she greedily tries to catch every last fucking drop of us.

I don't think life can get any better than this.

A beat passes, and we all just stand there staring at each other, before Kale drops to his knees, his hands darting up to grip her shoulders, easing her down until her back is resting on the ground. Kale's hand reaches out to cover Savannah's eyes before lifting his mask slightly, allowing him to give her what she wants.

Reign removes his mask and joins Kale, their tongues drawing languid strokes across her smooth skin, licking our hot cum from her body, just like she asked.

I say nothing.

I don't so much as move as I lose myself to the trance this sight before me has me under, until Savannah's voice pulls me back from my daze.

"Are you coming, big boy?" she teases, and the contentment and satisfaction in her voice makes everything about this moment feel even more right.

I drop to my knees, knowing there isn't a single thing I wouldn't do for this woman.

My best friend's tongues both tangle with mine, and we revel in the taste of our combined aftermath.

It's them, both of them, mixed with me, and I will never get enough.

Savannah's breaths are heavy, her every sensation magnified at this moment, and I slide my hand down her stomach, moving lower until I'm trailing my fingertips across her bare pussy. I slide a finger between her dripping heat, tracing soft circles along her clit, and she raises her hips, searching for more.

"Now, now, Little Viper," I whisper, removing my fingers away from her to tease her a little.

"Oh, no, *please*," she pleads, her eyes still covered with Kale's hand.

"Please don't stop. I don't think I can take it." *You don't have to ask me twice, baby girl.*

I sink my middle finger in deep, before slowly pulling back out, circling her clit with her arousal, my touch, soft and barely brushing against her sensitive flesh, but I know she feels me all the way to her bones.

Her pussy pulses beneath my touch, and the frustrated groan that leaves her lips is enough for me to want to bend her over and fuck her senseless.

She opens her mouth to speak, but her voice is cut off when I slam two fingers into her, causing her to buck against my hand. I pump my fingers in and out, and Reign's eyes are fixated on the spot where Savannah and I are connected. I see the decision flash across his face as he moves in closer, taking her clit into his mouth.

"Oh fuck. Fuck... *Fuck yes. Please don't fucking stop!*"

"Does she feel as good as we imagined she would?" Kale asks, his voice laden with desire.

"Even better," I murmur, staring down at Reign lapping at her while I finger her cunt.

Reign rises to meet my face, hovering before me, and he presses his lips to mine. Soft and gentle. His tongue darts out to part my lips, and I surrender easily. His tongue brushes against mine, and all I taste is Savannah.

He pulls back, his wide, dark eyes only looking at me for a split second before he shifts his gaze to her pussy, still filled with my fingers.

"Does this cunt want to be fucked?" he asks, and the corner of Kale's lips tilts into a half smile, knowing exactly what his twin is like, and what's about to happen.

I turn my hand upright, resting my palm against her clit, and fuck her hard and fast with my fingers.

"Y-yes," she finally answers, her voice trembling from my frantic movements.

"Yes, what?" Reign bites out.

"Yes, please. I want you all to fill me," she manages to say, and I pump up, hitting that sweet fucking spot, not making this conversation any easier for her.

"You want us all to fill *what? Say it*," he pushes, not letting her get away with being vague. He wants her to admit it. He needs to know all the dark and twisted things his little stepsister wants us to do to her, because we've spent years wanting—wishing that we could.

SEVEN

SAVANNAH

"You want us all to fill *what?*" the masked stranger demands, and I'm sorry, but I'm finding it a little hard to concentrate when his friend is fucking me with his fingers. I can't see a thing because of the hand covering my eyes, and it only adds to the euphoria.

I have never been fucked like this.

Correction.

They haven't even fucked me yet.

Still, if this is their version of foreplay, I've got to say, this is going to be the worst goodbye of my damn life because how the hell is a girl supposed to casually walk away from this? I don't ever want to let them go.

"I want you to fill my...*cunt*. I want you all to

fuck me. *Please.* I can't. I'm ready for it, just please don't stop," I whine, and with each word that I say, he fucks my pussy harder, the palm of his hand rubbing against my clit—I am so fucking desperate for release.

They're edging me, and as much as I love this, I have to feel their cocks inside me.

It's not a want at this point. *It's a need.*

My toes curl, and I move my hands in front of me, gripping the hair that belongs to the guy who's blocking my vision, and his tongue moves higher, licking their cum from my sensitive nipples.

I am going to hell. But, I've accepted that.

The whole *'ask and you shall receive'* thing really works, because if you told me that I'd be in the middle of the woods with three masked strangers, with no light but the moon to guide me, I'd have laughed in all your faces. But if you told me that I'd be witnessing a live fucking porno where three faceless strangers jerk each other off five inches from my eyes, covering me in their cum, right before all three of them fuck me into a coma, I'd have dropped dead.

Goodbye, me. You had a good life.

"That's a good girl," the stranger praises, obviously pleased that I'm a willing participant in this game we're all playing here.

The sound of movement fills my ears as whoever's fingers are inside me are removed, and I whine at the loss of contact. The hand that covers my eyes is the next thing to go, and I blink a few times, trying to re-adjust to the darkness. I look up, their shadows moving around me, and they each exchange a glance, and understanding of what's about to happen hits me.

Finally.

"I'm going to lie down, and I want you to sit on my lap, facing away from me, alright, baby?" the man closest to me says, and I obey. Slowly, I stand, turning to face him as he lies back, his clothes forgotten. My eyes rake over his large, muscular body, and Jesus fucking Christ, he's a sight to behold. The moonlight highlights the contours of his ripped torso, peppered with intricate tattoos. It's a little too dark for me to distinguish the ink fully, but it doesn't matter. You don't need eyes to know that he's hot.

He just is.

All of them are.

His arms stretch out, his hands moving to gesture for me to come closer, inviting me to sit on his lap. My body moves almost by instinct, and I can feel my pussy clench in anticipation. I turn, and his large hands guide my ass as I sit upright in his lap, facing away from him. His hard cock presses against my tight hole, and I grind my hips slowly, teasing him a little. Part of me doesn't want to look away from him, but when the others move in closer, wearing nothing but masks, I forget how to breathe.

"Lie back, baby. I want to feel your perfect body against mine," the guy beneath me says, his voice soft and alluring, which is a stark contrast to the gravelly, demanding tones the others have.

I lie back, but not all the way, realizing that he's moved forward a little, leaning back against his arm to support our bodies. He slowly runs his free hand over my skin, squeezing my breast, before moving lower, tracing his fingertips along my abdomen, before settling between my legs.

"I fucking love how wet you are for us," he says, barely above a whisper in my ear. And I let out a loud moan when he runs his middle finger through my pussy, then uses his index finger to spread me open. I didn't even notice the man in front of me, stroking his large cock at the sight of his friend, spreading my pussy for him.

"Fuck you look like an angel like this. So fucking ready for us. But you're not an angel, are you, Little Viper? You're a dirty little slut aching for our cocks to fuck you. You want us to devour you until there's nothing left for anyone else to claim, isn't that right?" he says, and I nod because what we are about to do is far from pure, and he's right. I want that so bad.

What we're doing is dirty, unholy even, but fuck if I'm going to stop them.

"I want you to fuck her, baby. I want you and our guy to fill both her tight holes, while I stuff her pretty little face with my cock." This comes from the man to my right, looking like a dark knight in the shadows as he strokes himself so close, yet so far away from my face.

I want him to destroy me.

I want *all* of them to.

"Is that what you want, Little Viper? I'm gonna need to hear you say the words."

"Yes. I want it. I want to feel you. *Please just fuck me.*" I don't even know what I'm saying, my head is all over the place, and all sense of logic has been replaced with the unrelenting need to be devoured in every way possible by them.

Without another word, the tall shadow closes the distance between us. The moon highlights parts of his strong, tattooed body, now engulfing mine, and I can feel the hard cock pressed against my ass twitch, rubbing his pre-cum along my skin as he thrusts against me, chasing friction.

I turn to face the man at my side, but a hand darts out, lightly gripping my chin with his thumb and index finger, turning me back to look up at him.

"I want you to look at me while I fuck you, Savy."

Savy?

Before I can process his words, the guy beneath me wraps his arm around my chest, pulling me back into him. His breaths are warm and heavy on my neck, his mask is not enough of a barrier to stop us from getting closer to each other. When his arm moves, I immediately miss his touch.

I don't even feel the cool weather with all the heat radiating throughout my body at the sight of the two masked men standing in the dark before me.

"Open," the man below me demands, and I do, sucking his large fingers into my mouth. "Get them nice and wet for me, baby girl." I do what he asks before his fingers pull out, then I feel it.

I gasp as he circles my sensitive hole with my own saliva. His fingers dance around before he slowly pushes the tip of his finger inside. A wave of goosebumps prickles my skin, and it's a feeling like I have never felt before.

He's going to fuck me in the ass.

He slowly teases my hole, stretching me, and

working me, getting me ready for him. The shadow before me moves, and I look to see him coat his own fingers with his spit, still stroking his cock. I gasp when I feel another finger enter me. The burn is strange at first, but I don't want him to stop.

"Need a little help?" The guy in front of me spits into his hand, then brings his fingers down to join his friend's.

Fuck.

He trails his saliva along the other guy's fingers before they're pushed back inside me, this time, knuckle deep. I already feel so fucking full, and I need him to move. I need him inside me right now, or I might just die.

"Please. Please, *I need,*" I beg on a gasp, but before I can continue, he pushes the tip of his cock against my asshole.

"Are you ready, baby?"

"Of course she's fucking ready. She's a greedy little bitch, aren't you, Savy?" The man calls me by my nickname again, and I open my mouth to ask how the fuck he knows it, but I'm completely caught off guard when my hole starts to stretch, and the tip that was just circling me is now burying inside.

It feels wrong, yet at the same time, I need him to fill me more.

"*Ohmyfuckinggod!*" I cry out, not making any sense, so I bite my lip to prevent myself from moaning something stupid. He pulls out a little, then gradually works his way back in, only this time, he bucks up into me deeper and deeper, until my ass is fully seated on his hard dick.

"Are you okay, baby?" he asks, his voice soothing and gentle. If I didn't know better, I'd say he genuinely cares about me, or at the very least, cares about how he's making me feel at this moment.

"Y-yeah. I'm okay. I just need you to move. *Please.* I need you to fuck me."

"*Fuuuck....*" he groans, before he lifts me by my ass cheeks, then slowly slides me back down onto him. My vision starts to blur at the corners, and I feel him all over my body as he begins to drive up into me. My moans fill the cool night air, and I'm fully conscious of the others' eyes on me. Observing me as I unravel on their friend's cock that's now fucking my ass.

After this, if I die, I'd be okay with it, because nothing I do from here on out will ever beat this moment.

He pulls me into him even more until I'm flush against his bare chest, then the shadow standing before me moves in closer, trailing the tip of his dick along my dripping pussy.

"I'm gonna fill you up, Savy. I'm gonna coat your pretty cunt with my cum because I know you've always wanted this. You're trapped and tangled in our web, Little Viper, and there's no escaping us now," he promises, his voice hoarse, and I can tell that he's barely holding on as he stares down at me. My every thought is hijacked when he slides his long, thick cock into my pussy, and all the breath leaves my lungs with how full I feel.

Thank God I'm on fucking birth control or we'd be having a completely different conversation.

He starts moving, thrusting his hips against me, fucking me so good. I stare up at him, his mask doing all kinds of naughty things to me as his breathing grows more rampant. His hands grip the back of my thighs, holding them higher, until I'm fully exposed to them. Their cocks slamming into both my holes.

"You feel so fucking good, I knew you would. You're fucking intoxicating, woman," the man fucking my pussy growls, and I can feel his sweat as it drips on my body from the exertion of making me his.

So fucking hot.

"Like a fucking dream," the man below me pants,

his breaths labored, before they lose all composure and start fucking me wilder, and harder until I'm floating right out of my body.

It's ethereal, the pleasure they're giving me, and I don't want this to be over.

"Give me that perfect, dirty fucking mouth," the guy to my right says, and I turn my head to face him, on his knees, waiting for me. His masked face is hidden by the night, but this is still the best thing I've ever seen in my life.

I open my mouth for him, and he fills it within seconds. I immediately get to work. I swirl my mouth around his swollen tip, tasting his pre-cum like it's some kind of prize for being a good fucking girl for them. Their low, breathy sounds have me teetering closer and closer to the edge.

"Baby, *ugh,* you feel–*ah!* You're taking us so well."

"Such a good fucking whore for us, Savy." Their voices only fuel me to keep sucking, and my muffled cries only drive my dark knight crazy. His hand reaches out, fisting my hair as he fucks my mouth senseless. Tears begin to trail down my face from the connection, and I realize that this is the first time anyone has owned me like this. Never have I been claimed like this before, but now that I have, I'm ruined for any other men for life.

"Savy, I'm gonna come. I-I'm coming," the guy fucking my pussy whines, rutting into me a few more times before he completely lets go. He comes, and comes hard, and my pussy clenches, my own release building with each final thrust.

"I'm coming! Fuck, I'm coming! Please don't fucking stop!" He growls at my words, mumbling something unintelligible before my pussy pulses, coming all over his cock. He slumps down, covering my body with his. He burrows his head in between my tits, but he doesn't pull out. He just stays like this while I suck the other guy's cock, our vulgar sounds echoing around us.

"Baby, I'm there."

"*I'm. so. fucking. there!*" the others say in unison, and within seconds, hot ropes of hot cum fill my mouth, and I can feel the large dick in my ass pulsate, as I squeeze every last drop from him.

"Swallow." I turn my head to face the masked man lying on my chest, looking up at me in the dark. "I said, swallow, Little Viper." I do just that. With a gulp, I swallow his friend's cum, then in seconds, I'm being lifted. The guy beneath me eases his cock out of me, and I feel totally fucking spent.

The man before me lifts me to my feet, the others moving around us. He gazes down at me through his mask, and I don't know what's happening. He simply holds me upright, probably making sure that my legs don't give out.

I can smell him.

I can smell all of them, and I could get drunk off just their scent alone. Leather, sex, and bad decisions, though it's too late for me to run from them now.

"Here." I turn my attention to the others, holding out a leather jacket for me.

"We destroyed your clothes, you'll need this." I take it from him, and the other helps me put it on. It swims on me, covering at least half of my thighs. I cross my arms, grateful that I get to take a souvenir home with me.

"Uhh… thanks," I finally say like an idiot. Who the hell says thanks after they've been fucked by three faceless strangers in the woods? I obviously do, because apparently, I don't know how to act around them now.

"Don't mention it," one of them says, handing me my phone.

"It was in your pocket, but I kinda destroyed your leggings, so…"

"Right, well. I should probably get back. I'm the designated driver." Before I embarrass myself any more than I already have, I turn and walk in the direction from which I came.

"We'll see you around, Little Viper. We'll always find you." I turn around, but they've vanished, hidden by the night.

Ghosts.

Gone but never forgotten, and all I have to show for tonight is their jacket... *and their cum dripping from my body.*

I switch on my phone, and a message pops up from River, sent about three minutes ago.

River Baby:

> Hey, Bitch, where did you go?
> Anyways, I'm waiting by the car. It's
> locked, so let me know when you're
> on your way. Hope you got laid xx
> kk bye.

Me:

> On my way, and, Bitch, you have
> nooo idea!

Pocketing my phone, I walk out into the clearing that backs onto the frat house. The hair on the back of my neck stands to attention. I look around, suddenly aware that I'm alone out here, when I see him.

Blake walks my way, and I immediately pick up the pace. I don't want to deal with this fucking asshole tonight. If he sees me like this, thoroughly fucked, I'll never hear the end of it. Even though he has no reason to talk.

"Vannah, wait up!" Agrh. I hate it when he fucking calls me that.

"What are you, a fucking toddler? My name is Savannah. I have nothing to say to you. We're over, Blake. Move on. Oh, wait, you already did. Tell Molly I said hi," I spit out, picking up the pace, but he grabs my arm from behind, spinning me around to face him.

"Let go of me! You're fucking hurting me!"

"Shut the fuck up, you stupid bitch. I'm sick to fucking death of you whining and complaining about every little thing. You can fucking stand here and hear me out." I go completely still.

My heart thumps heavily in my chest, and I try to clear my head, searching for a way to get out of this if it goes bad. He doesn't remove his hand from my upper arm. Instead, he squeezes tighter, staring down at me with the same expression he always does.

I'm realizing now that it's contempt that I see churning in his eyes, even if his features are hardly noticeable in the dark.

"You don't get to fucking break up with me, bitch. I fucking made you," he shouts, and I curse myself for flinching. He's fucking out of his goddamn mind, because we weren't together long enough for him to make me come, let alone '*make me*' anything else.

"You're drunk, Blake. Let's just talk about this tomorrow, okay?" His eyes rake over my body, and I stiffen. His eyes grow wide and threatening, and I inwardly brace myself for whatever happens next.

"Who did you fuck, Savannah?!"

I don't say anything. I can't even think with him holding onto me like this. He raises his other arm and grabs my hair. My skull burns as he pulls my head back, then his other hand wraps around my throat. "*Who. Did. You. Fuck?*" he rages, emphasizing each word. He's acting like a total fucking crazy person right now.

He's never done anything like this before.

I could lie, I suppose. I could say that someone spilled their drink all over me, and I had to borrow someone else's clothes to wear home. Though my makeup is probably all over the place, and it would be way too obvious that I was lying.

My heartbeat grows even more frantic as he tightens his grip on my throat.

"You're hurting me, Blake, *p-please*. Can we just talk about this tomorrow? I'm... I'm s-sorry, okay. I shouldn't have said that about Molly. Please, Blake. Just let me g-go," I say through ragged breaths, and he smiles. All signs of the guy I thought I knew are gone, replaced with someone unhinged and unrecognizable.

"I'll find out, Savannah, you know I will. And when I do, I'll kill your whore ass in front of them, because you weren't theirs to fuck. Do you hear me? Nobody wants you, Savannah. And the sooner you realize that I'm as good as you're gonna get, the easier life will be for you."

EIGHT
REIGN

She may not be able to see us, but we sure as fuck can see her and that stupid cunt! My anger is brimming, and the need to break every bone in his body is riding me harder than Jackson ever has, but if I rush out there now and play the protective stepbrother, she will know it was us that just fucked her brains out.

"I'm gonna kill that fucking piece of shit!" Kale snarls and moves fast, attempting to brush past us, but Jax and I manage to hold him back. "Get the fuck off me!" he seethes. His body is fucking vibrating with anger.

"Calm the fuck down, asshole! If you go out there right now, she is going to know what we did, and that can't happen." At Jax's words, he seems to calm, though only slightly.

"He's touching her," my twin grits out, his jaw locked tight, teeth clenched, and it only makes him look even more rabid as he watches Blake stand over her.

I place a hand on his chest and step into his view. "I know, brother, he will pay for touching what's ours, but not tonight." The look in his eyes, a mirror image of my own, is almost demonic. He's unhinged, and even though he tries to hide the devil inside him, I can see it. If we don't get Kale the fuck out of here now, he is going to kill Blake, and there won't be a damn thing we can do to stop him. He might be the romantic type, but my twin has a dark side. There's something dangerous caged beneath his surface, and none of us wants whatever it is to escape.

I peer over my shoulder just in time to see Blake release Savy with a forced shove. She loses her footing and falls to the ground, our jacket doing nothing to hide the perfectly fucked body now on full display to Blake.

Kale rages, and Jax and I have no choice but to drag my twin away. I feel like a fucking piece of shit for leaving her on the ground while he, of all people, stands above her, laughing at her like she's nothing more than shit beneath his shoes, but I can't risk Kale getting his hands on Blake.

For all of our sakes.

We've never liked that asshole, not even a little, and the moment he started dating our girl, our dislike transformed into pure fucking hatred. Every chance we get, we fucking drop his ass on the field. Accidents happen and all that jazz. Kale even managed to pop the cocksucker's shoulder out one time, but after what he's just done to our girl, he'd be lucky if he ever gets to fucking play football again when we're done with him.

* * *

The rest of the weekend is spent training and keeping a close eye on Kale. My brother is still itching to give Blake the beating he deserves, but that can't happen, not right now. Jax and I wanted to hunt Savy down and get another taste of her, but Kale is too on edge, and he isn't thinking straight. He'd blow our cover, and who knows what would happen then.

When Monday rolls around, he's still too wound up, so hunting our girl will have to wait. Blake started running his mouth at practice about him and Savy getting back together, and wouldn't shut his fucking mouth about it. That asshole said that he still planned to fuck Molly on the side, and while we don't care about open relationships, we know that their terms are nothing like ours.

Hearing that shit spit from Blake's mouth sent Kale into a tailspin, undoing whatever cooling off he had done over the past couple of days. He destroyed the locker room, and two of our tight ends had to help both Jackson and me drag him out of there before he murdered Blake's sorry ass in front of everyone.

The team captain has no idea how fucking lucky he is that we stopped my twin.

Kale has had an obsession with Savy for years now. I knew the moment he finally got his hands on her that shit would be different between all of us. There is no out for her now, and Blake is only tempo-rary, but part of me thinks she only took him back because he gave her no other fucking choice. Kale, Jackson, and I have claimed her, and we will do whatever the fuck it takes to keep her.

"I'm gonna kill that motherfucker!" Kale spits from the back seat of my car as we pull into the parking lot. So much for an average Wednesday morning. I look over and see Blake running after Savannah and River, and before my twin even thinks about leaving, I click the locks, trapping him in here with us.

"You've got to be fucking kidding me! Really, you fucking assholes?"

"Calm the fuck down, Kale!" Jackson snaps. "She's a big girl and can handle herself. You know, going out there right now and beating the shit out of him will raise questions none of us are willing to answer. Also, we can't risk her mom and your dad finding out about what we did." The joint in his hand seems to calm Kale down enough for him to stop clenching his fists like a goddamn fucking psycho.

The three of us remain silent as we sit and watch them. River smacks Blake's hand away, successfully stopping him from touching our girl. I knew we liked her for a reason. We can see that they're both pissed off, and it's obvious they both want him to fuck off and leave them alone, but he's a persistent mother-fucker. It only makes me think that I may be right. Maybe they didn't get back together after all. We didn't know they had broken up in the first place, but that didn't stop us from claiming her on Halloween night.

Blake is a spoiled rich kid who thinks he's better

than everyone, and the fact that Savy dumped his ass is fucking with his ego.

"If he lays another fucking finger on her, I'm gonna kill him. How the fuck are you both so okay with this?"

Call me fucking crazy, but I believe my brother would actually do it, and it would only ruin his fucking life. As much as I want the asshole dead, I can't let my brother be the one to do it. I won't live without my twin.

By the time Friday rolls around, Kale seems a lot less like a serial killer and more like the cool, calm, and collected guy we all know and love. We have a family dinner with our dad and Savy's mom on Saturday, so we have a plan to follow her back to her dorm after, and finally hunt her fine little ass down and fuck her so hard she forgets her own fucking name.

Kale left practice early today and never said a word to me or Jax, which has me on edge. My twin never goes off and does shit on his own, especially not without telling one of us, but Jax told me to leave him be. He said that he needs to get his head straight so he's calm and not so obvious about his need to protect her. *Or fuck her.* The thought of touching her again has me rock hard and brimming with need, and

I can't fucking wait to have her again. Jesus, I won't be able to wait until tomorrow.

I need a fucking release now.

I wait for the locker room to clear, and once the last person leaves, I lock the door and head straight to the showers, where I know Jackson is. His back is to me as I enter, and the sight of his muscles glistening beneath the hot water has me fucking salivating. I strip off my gear quietly, not taking my eyes off his firm, tight ass, and then go in for the kill, not wasting any fucking time.

I have to have him.

Gripping the back of his neck, I force him forward until his front is plastered against the cold tiled wall. He grunts from the force of my body and looks back at me from the corner of his eye.

"I've been fucking hard for you all day," he purrs, and I bury my face in the crook of his neck, not holding back the groan that creeps up my throat from his words. I grind my cock against his ass and relish in the moan that slips free from his lips. I reach around his front with my free hand and fist his cock. "Fuck, Reign," he hisses when I squeeze, feeling him harden with my touch.

"You like that, don't you, you fucking cock hungry whore?" I sneer.

He presses his ass against me, and I bite my lip to keep from moaning too loud. "I need to feel you inside me, *now*."

Music to my fucking ears.

I bite down on the soft flesh between his shoulder and neck, and he cries out in pain. His cock twitches in my hand, and that's the only green light that I need. Jackson loves it rough and dirty, and hearing him bark orders last week and take control as we fucked Savy had me so damn hard for him.

"Hands on the wall, you dirty slut." He places his palms flat against the wall, then I release him, lowering to my knees. I part his cheeks, growing even harder at the sight of him like this, then spit on my fingers before swirling them around his tight asshole. I fucking love the sounds coming from him. All needy and breathy for me. "You will always be our dirty little secret, Jackson. Nothing and no one will ever change what we have."

He looks back as I climb to my feet, and when I press my cock into him, his breath hitches, his green eyes glazing over in anticipation of what's to come.

"Fuck me, Reign, and show me how much you want me, baby."

God fucking dammit.

Unable to control myself, I thrust into him. I

don't have it in me to take this slow. I moan while his whimpers fill the empty locker room, echoing around us, and it drives me fucking wild.

"Take my cock, you slut," I snap, drawing back only to thrust into him again, but this time even harder.

"Yes, give me every fucking inch of you, Reign, baby," he pants out, his mouth hanging open as he takes me so fucking well.

"Lean forward," I bark, and he pushes his ass out and bends over, giving me better access. At this angle, I can fuck him deeper, just the way he likes it. "Fist your cock, baby. I want to fucking hear you scream my name as I fill this ass with my cum." Jackson obeys without complaint, and *fuck,* the sight of him pleasuring himself with my hard fucking dick in his ass nearly pushes me over the edge. I fight against the need to come, needing to savor this fucking moment with him. Each time that we fuck, he and I get closer and closer to each other, and it's not often I get to have him like this, all to myself without my twin's dick in his mouth or vice versa.

The three of us are dysfunctional. I won't deny it. Yet, there is an unbreakable bond between all of us that nobody has ever tried to understand. No other girl has accepted us for who we are, and whenever we've invited a woman into our circle, for lack of a better word, they always tried to push one of us out, and that's never going to fucking happen. The other night, when we were all together, something shifted between us. Between all of us. I know that Savannah would never judge us for wanting to fuck each other. In fact, it's quite the opposite. She wanted whatever it was we were willing to give her, and it set us all on fire.

"Fuck, Reign, baby, *I'm so close*," Jax moans, his voice all raspy from being fucked.

I reach up and tangle my fingers in his short black hair the best I can, tugging on the strands the way he likes it. "Me too, baby. Be a good little cum slut and wait for me. Can you do that for me?"

"Y-Yes, babe. Oh, fuck. I need to come with you. *Please.* I want to feel you fill my hole with your cum until it drips from my fucking body."

Fuck. That mouth of his will be the ruin of me.

The motherfucker knows that his dirty fucking words are a weakness for me, and I won't be able to fight against the pull that threatens to take me under.

"Get there, Jax. C'mon, baby, I'm about to come!" I sob, my every fucking fiber burning with the need to fill him.

"I'm there, love. I'm so fucking there. Please.

Make me come with you. *Ugh, Reign... Reign baby, fuck yes!"*

I am dead.

I thrust into him three more times, and then we're both roaring each other's name like a fucking prayer. Being with Jackson like this is fucking electrifying, and I don't think I'll ever get enough of him. Shudders roll through me as I empty everything I have inside him, and he squeezes every last fucking drop like it's a damn cure.

Jackson is more than just our best friend.

He is the first person Kale and I have ever been in love with.

Yeah, that's right. We're in love with Jackson Graves.

I pull out of him slowly, jerking a little with how sensitive my spent cock is, then reach up to grip his shoulders and spin him around. I shove him against the wall and claim his mouth, kissing him so that he knows who fucking owns him. He instantly melts into me, his tongue dancing along mine as he grips my waist like I'm his anchor. He holds me like I am his reason, and I've never said the words, but he's my fucking reason, too.

Before he can deepen the kiss, I pull back and gaze into his eyes. So green and beautiful that I might just get lost in them. "You're mine, Jackson. You may submit to me in moments like this, but never give up the control that I know you've got hidden in here." I shift my hand and place it in the center of his chest before continuing. "Whenever our girl is concerned, you let him out, baby, because that shit had me and Kale so fucking weak for you. The way that you took control, owning her, owning us... I want more, Jax."

The fucker chuckles, reaching up to brush away the wet hair stuck to my face. "I give you both the control you crave because it gets me off, but I'll never hand that shit over where she is concerned. She is mine in the same way that you and Kale are, yet different. She is mine to make submit, just as I am to you and your brother," he says, and the grin on his face is everything. Then, he pushes me back, shooting me a wink as he stalks out of the showers, my laughter following after him.

I make quick work of washing myself before gathering my gear off the floor and heading back to my locker to change. I freeze when I see Jax standing there. His fists are clenched tightly, but it's the pale look on his face that has terror rolling through me.

"Where's my brother?" I ask without thought.

He lifts his gaze to me, and the fear in his eyes

has my chest tightening as dread sinks its claws deep into me. He shakes his head, unable to form any words, and turns his phone to me so I can read the text.

Kale:

> I fucked up, Jax, I couldn't let it go.
> I need your help.

The message alone is ominous, but the image that he sent after it has all the blood draining from my face. Panic like I have never felt before is setting in. It takes me five minutes to form the words I need to.

"We take this to our fucking graves, Jackson. No one can fucking know about this, do you hear me? Fucking no one." The world moves fast around me as I stare down at my best friend. His eyes are vacant as he stares back. "Let's go help my brother cover up a murder."

NINE

SAVANNAH

I can still feel the ghost of them inside me.

I lie awake in bed, reliving that night in the woods alone with them. I'm not ashamed to admit that I've used my Satisfyer Pro so many times this week, just to curb my need for them, but it's not enough. I don't think I'll ever get them out of my system. I've spent every waking moment since wishing they'd find their way to me, to dominate me, and force me to obey their every command.

River tried convincing me to go out with her tonight, but I politely turned her down. I'm not going anywhere. What if the masked men show up at my dorm room, hoping to fuck me, and I'm not even there? Thanks, but I'm not missing that for the world. I'd much rather spend my Friday night being used like a fuck doll than going out drinking and dancing.

My phone pings beside me, and I roll my eyes. River's probably pestering me, hoping that I've changed my mind, but when I swipe open the message, I realize that it's from an unknown number.

Unknown:

> You thought we forgot about you, didn't you?

Me:

> Who is this?

Unknown:

> C'mon, Little Viper, you know who it is. Now be a good little whore and follow the instructions, because if you make us wait, we won't let you come.

My breath hitches, and my body starts to tremble with longing as I reply.

Me:

> What instructions?

Unknown:

> You'll get them soon. You have
> twenty minutes, Little Viper.

Oh my God.

I force myself to focus, and I climb out of bed as fast as I can. I run around my room like a madwoman, trying to find something sexy to wear. When my phone pings again with another text, I leap across the room, anticipation at seeing them again taking over me.

They drop me a pin to their location, and my eyes widen. If I don't leave right this second, I'll be late. I grumble when I look down at the oversized band hoodie I'm wearing, and curse myself for deciding that today of all days would be a perfect fucking day to wear nothing but a pair of black Spanx underneath.

"Fuck it." I sigh, then shove my feet into my Docs, snag my keys off the hook, and rush out the door like my ass is on fire. The drive to the location goes by in a blur because I'm so excited to see my guys again. I need them even more than they made me need them on Halloween night.

I pull into the parking lot, and I'm a little confused as to why they told me to come here of all places. No one uses this end of the beach due to the amount of rips, and it's completely closed off and locked to the public. I pull out my phone to text them. Am I in the right place? If I've fucked up and I miss out on seeing them, I'll die, I swear to fucking God. A text comes through, interrupting my raging thoughts.

Unknown:

> Follow the track to your right and don't stop until we tell you to.

I swallow audibly and climb out of my car. The excitement I felt earlier lessens as I begin my trek through the woods that border the beach, and as I walk further into the trees, darkness envelopes me. A strong sense of foreboding washes over me, and the hair on the back of my neck raises. Anyone could be out here, and I'd have no way of knowing until it's too late.

I can feel eyes watching me, and I know that someone is out there, but I can't see them. It's overcast, which means that I don't have the light of a full moon to guide me as I walk into the darkness like I did on Halloween night.

The cool wind picks up, and I'm cursing myself for my useless fucking outfit. It's November now, which means it's starting to get fucking cold. Yet, my body shivers for reasons that have nothing to do with the weather.

Awareness and a mix of anticipation twists around me, and my pussy begins to throb. The feeling of being afraid has always had an effect on me, but I can't help it. It just does something to me. There is no better turn on than knowing that they're out here somewhere waiting for me, and I can't wait for whatever they have planned for me this time.

I continue along the path they told me to follow, and it seems to go on for fucking ever. I place one foot in front of the other, hoping I don't fall in some sand, sink hole, or some shit.

Everything is quiet, and the only sounds I hear are from my own footfalls and the waves crashing hard against the rocks and shoreline.

Just when I begin to think I've been misled, I see the faint glow of a fire up ahead.

I use the light as my guide, stepping out of the tree line, and I immediately cover my nose with my cold hands.

Something smells off.

Is someone burning rubber?

"*Little Viper, Little Viper.*" I whirl around on my

heels, blinking to focus my eyes through the darkness, hoping to spot them, but I see nothing.

"Why am I here?" I call out, and I figure that if I get them talking, maybe I can work out where the hell they are.

The waves roar loudly as they crash against the cliffside, and my heart starts to race.

Did I make a horrible mistake by coming out here on my own?

"Because we have a surprise for you," another voice calls out, a little raspier than the other's, only this time, it's coming from my other side.

The darkness does nothing to hide the fact that their eyes are all over me, because I can still feel them. The pressure of being their sole focus has the tiny hairs all over my body standing at attention, but I can't tell you how intoxicating it is to feel this way.

Is it crazy to feel so wanted, even without them actually saying it?

It's in the way they show me.

Use me.

Taste me.

It's in everything they do to me.

Never have I felt so worshipped.

Blake doesn't give a single fuck about me. He only cares about himself and his image, which is why

I've spent the past week trying to get the fuck away from that psycho asshole.

I shake away all thoughts of Blake Humphreys because I won't let him ruin another great night for me.

"Is the surprise having all three of you inside me again?" I taunt, and the sound of their laughter sends a wave of warmth all over my cold body.

"Not tonight."

What? No!

Disappointment thrums through me as another voice draws out from behind me. These guys are fucking everywhere and nowhere at the same time.

"Tonight is about punishment."

Oh God.

Goodbye disappointment, hello excitement.

I can't explain the feeling that hits me when one of the guys steps out from the shadows, his skull mask in place. The mask alone should have me running, but it doesn't. It only adds to the heat already building inside me, and I hope they were lying about not fucking me.

The light from the fire casts an eerie amber glow across his tall, commanding frame, and the fact that he's towering over me only gives me chills.

I don't move as he slowly approaches me, his

shoulders broad and solid beneath his fitted black T-shirt. His tattoos trail up over his arms, disappearing beneath his shirt and preventing me from studying them properly. His body is to fucking die for, and the closer he gets, the harder my pussy begins to throb.

This is the first time I'm seeing them in actual lighting, and all I can think about is repeating everything we did last time, so that I can see them jerk each other off again in its full capacity.

He stops right in front of me, and I crane my neck back to maintain eye contact.

Fuck he's tall. He's at least 6-foot-3. Being only 5-foot-2, almost everyone is taller than I am, but this guy takes the fucking cake.

I inhale sharply when I feel two other bodies close in behind me. I feel so small like this. Standing in the center of the three of them, but not in a bad way. They're like my wall of security, and I hate to admit it, but as I stare up at the guy in front of me, I picture Jackson. In my mind, it's him standing there, wanting me like the man in the skull mask wants me. And the two men standing behind me, I wish that they were Reign and Kale, because I want them to want me, too. So fucking badly.

They aren't them, Savannah. Just drop it.

River was right. I'm never going to get over them.

How can I? I'm surrounded by hot as fuck masked men, fulfilling my every fucking fantasy, and I'm thinking about them, wishing that these guys were my stepbrothers and Jackson, not three strangers.

I look away, annoyed at myself for getting all up in my head. I gasp when an arm wraps around my waist, and I'm pulled backward until I'm flush against a hard chest. One of the guys moves over to stand before me, and he leans down to look me in the eyes. His green eyes are visible through the mask, and I start to tremble in his hold.

"Tonight, one of us will face a punishment," he says, his voice low and rough.

"W-why?" I stutter.

"He broke a rule, now he has to watch his brother fuck you." *Um. Excuse me?* My eyes widen at his declaration. Does he mean brother as in friend, or brother as in *brother*? I groan as an image of Reign and Kale flashes through my mind, but before I can get too lost in my thoughts, he releases his hold on me and pushes me forward, causing me to collide with the man standing off to the side. His hands instinctively grip my waist, and he spins me around so that my back is to his chest. I feel his warmth immediately, and I don't want him to let me go.

I stare at the other, wondering what the fuck is

going on, but my train of thought is derailed when a hand starts to move tentatively across my hip.

Oh my.

He runs his hand across my stomach before he slides it underneath the fabric and inside my pants. "Here's what's gonna happen. His punishment is to watch me fuck you, and you... you are going to be a good fucking girl for me, Little Viper. Understand?" he says seductively, his warm breath teasing, sending a wave of goosebumps across my skin.

"I understand."

The guy on the right clenches his fists at his sides, the mask doing very little to hide the rage boiling beneath his surface.

"I'm gonna break your fucking neck for this," he spits. The man with the green eyes grabs his arms and holds him back, but their attention is on the hand slipping inside my panties. My thoughts are a jumbled mess as he cups my pussy, and I bite my tongue to prevent myself from crying out.

"Fuck, her pussy is already dripping into my hand, brother," he teases, and the green-eyed guy drags the other one backward, almost bucking as he fights against him.

"Hey, you watch him fuck our girl. I promise I'll go easy on you." The instant his words sink in, the guy stops fighting. His demeanor has completely changed, and my breathing turns ragged as the man cupping my aching pussy pushes a finger inside me.

I rise onto my tiptoes, my body immediately reacting to his touch.

"You're a dirty fucking girl, Savy. You're already trying to milk my finger with that pretty tight cunt of yours, and I've barely even touched you… yet." *I love it when he calls me that.* My mind is reeling, and my body is on fire, as need and desperation course through me like a wildfire that can't be extinguished.

I feel like I'm going to combust when the two guys in front of me grab each other and start ripping their clothes off.

Please, God, make them tear their masks off too, so I can see their faces.

Even in their haste to undress, they are careful not to knock their masks out of place, and I don't hold back the pout on my lips at the disappointment.

"Look at how hard their cocks are." My eyes drop to the spot between their legs and they widen when I see that they're both rock hard and ready for each other. They throw their clothes to the sand, situating themselves to watch me get fucked.

It's hard to focus with the finger fucking my pussy like he owns it. Right now, I would tell this man anything, just so he would make me come. I don't want to be edged. Not tonight.

Moans tumble from my lips when he pushes his free hand under my hoodie and begins twisting my nipple between his fingers. I watch the others, not wanting to take my eyes from them as one of the guys is shoved onto his hands and knees, while the other crouches behind him, spanking his ass hard.

"*Fuck,*" I hiss, and then he presses his thumb against my sensitive clit, circling it ever so slowly. *Such a tease.*

"Do you want to come on my fingers or my cock, Little Viper?" he purrs and grinds his hips into my ass, and I can feel how hard he is.

"Cock!" I pant, and I don't care if they can see how gone I am for them. He chuckles, and I can tell that '*cock*' was the answer he was hoping for, and he better reward me for being a good girl and choosing the right option, because right now, not coming for him isn't fucking happening. I need this release more than I need my next fucking breath, especially when I have to watch the two in front of me fucking like their lives depend on it.

"Take your fucking clothes off, then get in the same position as my boy."

I don't need to be told twice.

I do as he says, and remove my clothes from my body faster than a damn rocket. Once I'm naked, everyone stops moving. Their eyes rake over my naked body, their own bodies now rigid as they greedily take me in.

I don't bother hiding from them. Instead, I decide to have a little fun of my own just to help push them over the edge.

They need to be reminded of who is really in charge here. While I love our little games, at the end of the day, I call the shots and they fucking know it.

I skate a single finger down my body all slow and sensual like, and when I reach my wet pussy, I glide my middle finger through my heat before pushing it inside. A loud moan escapes my lips, and I could have sworn that I heard all three of them whimper.

Hold onto your cocks, boys, because I'm not done.

Slowly, I slide my finger in and out, my mouth opening on a gasp as I add another finger. I can hear their low, breathy murmurs, and it only spurs me on. I remove my fingers from my pussy, then I bring them to my lips. I trail them along my bottom lip before wrapping my tongue around both of them, sucking them clean.

"*You dirty fucking bitch*, get the fuck into position now because I'm about to punish that cunt of yours for teasing me." I fight so fucking hard not to smirk, as I kneel, deciding that it's probably best that I do as he says. I lock eyes with the man in the same position as me, and feeling courageous, I slowly crawl forward across the sand, and I don't stop until his masked face is but a breath away from me.

I stare at the skull mask, studying the details, and when my eyes land on his, I hold his gaze. I watch as the firelight dances in his eyes, and for the first time, I truly see them. They are like golden honey, and they're actually beautiful, and when they drop to my lips, I can hear his mouth open, so I lick my lips on instinct.

We stay like this for a beat, staring into each other's eyes, then I get distracted when the guy behind me starts to massage the globes of my ass, smoothing his large hands up my lower back, before coming back down hard to slap my cheeks. I moan, jerking forward, and my face brushes up against Mr. Honey's mask.

I wish that I could kiss him, and I can see in his eyes that he so desperately wants to.

"Do you want his cock in your pussy, baby girl?" the guy before me asks, running his eyes over my face.

"Yes." I don't hesitate with my answer, because I

think it's safe to say that we're past that stage in our relationship—situationship, or whatever the fuck this thing is. They're willing to give me what I want, and I'm not in the business of pretending like I don't know what that is. I'm a big girl, and it feels like a waste of time not letting them do what they want to me, especially knowing that once this is over, they'll go back to their lives, wherever that is, and I'll go back to wishing they took me with them.

"Keep your eyes on me the whole fucking time and you don't come until I say you can come, got it?"

My jaw unhinges, and I open my mouth to reply, but the words die on my tongue when I feel the thick, hard cock pressing against my entrance. I thought that his watching me was supposed to be a punishment, but the glee swirling around those honey irises as his brother shoves his dick into my pussy, shows me that he's enjoying every fucking minute of it.

TEN

KALE

I watch as my brother slams inside her, making her scream so loud she could wake the dead body swimming below the cliff.

Good-fucking-riddance.

This woman, this beautiful fucking woman, has the power to make me see red without even trying, and when I see her like this, unravelling before my fucking eyes, I feel like it was all worth it.

I lost my mind today.

I spent the last week stuck inside my head worrying about Savannah with that fuckhead Blake. One thing led to another, and I fucked up. *Badly.*

Well, not so much for me, but very fucking badly for him. He'll be fish shit in no time, and it's what that fucker deserves for laying a hand on my girl.

I won't lie and say that I didn't panic, because of course I fucking did. Not because I killed him, but because I had no idea how to get rid of his body alone without being caught. So, naturally, I had to call for backup.

I expected them to lose their shit, but they didn't. Instead, they understood and helped me clean up the mess.

However, there were... *terms*.

I was to be punished, and I'm currently in the process of serving it as we fucking speak.

I never thought my punishment would be watching my mirror fucking image ravage the girl I'm in love with, much less fuck her right in front of my face. I also didn't think I'd have to watch them while Jax fucks me in the ass.

I am not usually the bottom.

That's Jackson's domain. But here I am, on my hands and knees, my ass in the air, waiting to get fucked by my best friend, all because I lost control.

I raise my right hand from the sand, and I move my arm back behind me to grip Jackson's waist, pushing up against my body. I dig my fingers into his skin, hard enough that I know I'll leave bruises, and if I'm being honest, I can't find it within myself to give a fuck. He is going to take the brunt of my anger because not being allowed to touch my girl is fucking ridiculous. Who even fucking made this rule?

My dick is so hard that it's almost painful, and all I fucking want to do is feel my woman.

My thoughts are interrupted when Jax spreads my cheeks apart, and he spits on my asshole.

"Dude?" I scold, but Jax just chuckles, before rubbing his cock against my rim.

"I'm gonna fuck you now, baby. I need you to relax for me, alright? You know the drill."

I look ahead, fixating on our gorgeous woman as she watches us intently. Then, in one swift movement, Jackson thrusts hard enough inside me that I almost go cross-eyed from the burn.

"Ja-*baby*." I almost fucking say his name, but quickly correct myself, not able to focus on anything but this feeling. It's all too much, yet not enough at the same time. I hold his hip tighter for support, hoping he doesn't make me headbutt our girl. Jax loves it hard and rough, and Savannah sure as shit knows it by now. The feeling of him being inside me is out of this fucking world, and when he starts to really pump into me, finding his rhythm, my cock grows even harder. I lock eyes with my twin, moaning and panting as he fucks Savannah like he's starving for it.

"She feels so fucking good, brother," the asshole taunts, and I grind my teeth to the point of pain with jealousy. I'm not jealous because he's fucking her, I'm jealous because I am not.

Jax thrusts into me harder, and the sound of skin slapping against skin echoes around us as we all fuck. Savannah whines, her grey-blue eyes fixated on me as we both succumb to overwhelming pleasure. Her long white hair falls in her face, and Reign bunches it up in his fist, then pulls her head back roughly.

"Tell him what he's missing out on, Savy. Tell him how fucking good my hard dick feels fucking your wet pussy so deep," Reign says, his breathing is all over the place as he submits to the euphoria of this moment. What a fucking asshole.

I look back at our girl, and I've never seen anyone so fucking sexy, so blissed out from being devoured. "Tell him, love." My mouth opens wide, and I can almost bet that Reign's does too.

He's never called a woman *love* before, and I think he's just as shocked as I am about it. I know that other people use it all the time, but not us. The word means something to us, and we don't give that shit to just anybody.

"His cock feels so fucking good pumping my pussy like this." My cock twitches at her lust-filled tone, and I seethe, wishing it were me behind her, not my fucking brother.

"Ah, fuck. Please fuck me harder," I beg, and I'm surprised at myself for wanting this, wanting him to fuck my ass so fucking bad. Picking up the pace, Jax ploughs into my hole rough and fast, and I can't hold back my groans. My face falls to the sand, my cheek pressing against the earth as his cock drives me wild.

"Do you like that, baby?"

"Yeah, I fucking love it!"

"Do you like being a good fucking bottom for me?" My body is on fire, my balls heavy and aching, and they desperately need draining. "Answer me or I'll stop."

"Y-*yes*. I love being a good bottom for you, baby."

"That's what I fucking thought," he says before he pulls out of me abruptly, then he moves around me, my hand brushing along his body as I release his hip.

My brows furrow as I try to make sense of what's happening. "Get up." I do as he says, not sure what the plan is here, but when he lies on the ground in front of me, in front of Savannah, my cheeks heat with... embarrassment. Because I think I know what he wants me to do.

"Now bounce on my fucking cock while you watch your brother fuck our girl."

He wants me to do *what?*

I've never done that before.

Letting go of my restraint, I crawl over his body, straddling his hips. I just know that this asshole is wearing a smug grin beneath his mask, because he says nothing as he waits for me to start.

"All a-fucking-board, love. I need you to ride me, right the hell now." I rise on my knees a little, reaching back to grip his hard dick, lining him up, and then I slowly ease down onto him.

"Ugh, baby," Jackson says on a groan, as I fully seat myself on his hard length. I look up to see Savannah, looking like a fucking dream, glowing so perfectly in the fire's amber light. Her eyes are wide, her mouth gaping open as she stares at my tattooed naked body. She looks up, her brows furrowing in pleasure as I start to move my hips, grinding on the rock-hard dick in my ass. This is a whole other level of intimacy. I feel so fucking full in this position, rocking my hips back and forth, before I need more. I need to feel more.

"Brother, *please.* I need..."

"You want her?" Is he fucking stupid? Of course I fucking want her.

"You bet your fucking ass I do," I say through ragged breaths as I grind harder on Jackson's dick. Then, within a matter of seconds, Reign pulls away from Savannah, and her brows pull together in confusion.

"Savy, love," Reign says, his voice soothing and gentle. A tone I have only ever heard him use a few times with Jackson.

"Yes?" she answers, her voice all husky and groggy, and it only makes my cock twitch.

"I saw that," Jackson teases, and I look down at him, and force as much annoyance in my expression as possible, so hopefully he can see it through the fucking mask.

"Shut the fuck up," I spit, but he just chuckles in response. I'm too afraid to say anything. I'm not supposed to be getting any fucking pussy tonight, and I fear that if I open my big mouth, I'll ruin whatever is about to happen here.

"Can we trust you, Little Viper?" I watch Savannah as she ponders that thought, before she nods her head in agreement.

"Of course you can trust me," Savannah says, her face filled with curiosity and want.

"Good, because he's going to take off his mask to eat his ass while you fuck both our cocks." Reign gestures to me, and I swear to fuck, a choir of angels starts singing in the distance. Reign helps Savannah to her feet, and my eyes fall to her swollen pussy.

She is fucking perfect.

It's like she was made for us.

"Savy, I want you to take a seat on his cock, while pretty boy over here sits on his face." Reign gestures to Jax and helps Savannah get situated. She looks down at me, her eyes wild with impatience.

Our dirty girl wants to come.

I unmount Jax's dick, feeling empty as all fuck the minute his cock leaves my ass. I allow Reign the room to help Savannah climb on top of Jackson, her beautiful tits bouncing with each of her movements. She's a goddamn temptress, that's what she is, and she has no fucking idea what she does to the three of us.

"That's a good girl," Jax croons, his hands now on her hips as she slides her pussy down his cock. Then, Reign walks behind her and lies down, his legs spread on either side of Jackson's body.

"She's gonna ride both our cock's like this, aren't you, Little Viper?"

"Yes, please. If you make me wait any longer, I'll cry," she replies, her gaze never leaving mine. I watch as Reign and Jax lift her ass, making enough room for

Reign to slide his cock inside Savannah's wet cunt, and her eyes roll to the back of her head.

"I-I feel so fucking full. You're stretching me."

"That's right, love. Our cocks are going to stretch you so fucking good. Ride us, baby," Reign's voice is hoarse and tense as both his and Jackson's dicks rub against each other. I take this moment to move closer, stepping over Jax's face before I bend my knees, crouching over him, and I'm fully aware of how exposed to him I am in this position.

Two things happen at once. Jackson removes his mask and wastes no time before he starts licking me. His tongue dancing around my asshole like he's starving for it, and my cock is fucking weeping. I'm face to face with the woman I love, riding their cocks so well. She's so fucking filthy, but in the best way. Her full tits bounce with each of their thrusts, and it's almost like they're in slow motion, a breath away from my face. Savannah is glowing. She's in her element like this, glowing like an angel in the orange light.

"This is the part where we learn if we can trust you or not, Savannah," Reign says, his breath labored as he thrusts hard into her pussy.

"You can trust me, I swear it."

"Close your eyes, baby," Jax instructs, and I

watch in awe as she obeys him without a second thought. "Don't open your eyes until we tell you to, am I clear?"

"Yes. I won't. I promise." When Savannah's eyes squeeze shut, Jax taps my hip, and I immediately remove my mask. I move in closer to her face, and God, she's so fucking beautiful. I raise my arm to grip her chin with my thumb and index finger, holding her still for me.

Then, I kiss her.

My stepsister.

The forbidden fruit we were never meant to taint, but so desperately craved.

My tongue darts out to part her lips, swollen and soft, and she opens her mouth, inviting me in. She kisses me back with as much longing and hunger as I feel, before all gloves are off.

It's a fucking collision.

Feverish and bruising, violent and healing, as our tongues tie together for the first time since I first laid eyes on her. I catch her bottom lip between my teeth when Jax pushes a finger inside me, then starts pumping in and out, his tongue still tasting me as he does it. She moans into my mouth as they fuck her harder, and I take this moment to pull away.

"Keep your eyes closed, Savannah." She nods,

and I trail soft kisses along her jaw, then down her neck, causing goosebumps to blanket her skin.

"You're gonna ruin me," she gasps, and we all chuckle at the same time. I wrap my tongue around her earlobe, slowly sucking it into my mouth, and she cries out. They fuck her harder, wilder, as she moans, and it's the hottest thing I've ever fucking seen in my life. I trail my tongue back down along her neck, then leave wet traces across her collarbone, before I reach out and squeeze her perfect tit.

Not wanting to be left out, she reaches for my cock, hard as fucking nails, then starts stroking me while Jackson fingers my ass even faster. Her eyes are still shut, but I focus on her mouth, and my weeping dick leaks pre-cum all over Jackson's chest as she fists my dick tighter.

"You feel so fucking good with your pussy wrapped around my cock, Little Viper," Reign says, and he's almost fucking growling as he bucks into her cunt.

"You taste so fucking good, baby," Jax says to me on a moan, and Savannah starts grinding back and forth, unashamedly, chasing her release. She pumps my cock harder, and I can't even breathe. It feels so fucking good. The wind and the waves are no match for the sound of our skin smacking against each other. Our moans are loud as we frantically fuck, and I don't ever want this moment to end.

I killed for her.

Hell, I'd fucking do it again.

She is worth everything, and when she finally comes, my twin and our best friend come undone, and so do I.

We chase our release together.

"That's it, Savannah. Fist my cock. Please don't fucking stop!"

"I won't fucking stop, baby. I want to make you come for us."

She just called me baby.

She beats my cock with her fist, hard and fast, until there's nothing fucking left of me.

I come, and come, riding Jax's fingers while she pumps me a few more times.

Hot ropes of cum spill all over our hot, joined bodies, writhing against one another, holding each other in a desperate rhythm as we fall more and more off the edge. Her lips curve into a proud smile, satisfied with her quest to get me there.

"Such a good fucking girl."

"I'm gonna come! *Please...* right there! I-I'm so fucking there!" Savannah screams, and the look on her face as she comes all over their cocks is fucking art.

This woman is mesmerizing.

"Your cock feels so fucking good against mine, baby," Jax says to my brother, and he's almost fucking sobbing as he finds his release.

"Your cock drives me crazy. And our dirty little slut fucked us so good, didn't she?" Reign growls, moaning and mewling beneath Savannah and me, before he comes inside her, coating Jackson's dick with his release. Everything goes quiet, and after a beat, I put my mask back in place. Jax removes his fingers from my ass, putting his mask back on as well.

Cum coats our sweaty bodies, and I wouldn't have it any other way. This was the best form of punishment, and I know that my twin gave her mouth to me as a gift. He knew I wanted to kiss her. And fuck, it was the best kiss I've ever had.

We are all just a tangled fucking mess, but I love how we are.

This is us.

This is what we become when we're together.

I only wish she could see who we really are beneath these masks.

ELEVEN

SAVANNAH

I could kiss my stepbrothers!

Thanks to them cancelling dinner with our parents, I was able to meet up with my masked men again on the following Saturday night, and every night for the past two weeks since. Each time we're together, it just keeps getting better and better. They chased me through the woods, all the way back to my dorm room, and cornered me after the football game. They fucked me senseless in the parking lot, and the fact that anyone could have seen us made it even hotter.

On the plus side, Blake has dropped off the face of the earth, and according to the rumors around campus, he's missing. If you ask me, he's just hiding away somewhere, licking his wounds because I dumped him, even if it took a while for it to sink in.

Yet, that isn't even the worst part. Molly Akers approached me last week and admitted that she and Blake had been hooking up for months! I'm not surprised. Though it seems she has bigger problems. Apparently, she's pregnant, and she told Blake the news the morning he went missing. No one has seen or heard from him since.

Fuck that guy.

I should feel angry, jaded, or even a little upset about him cheating, not to mention her pregnancy, but I feel nothing. Nothing but the ghost of my guy's cocks inside me. I mean, Jesus fucking Christ, they are unbelievably hot, and they treat me better than Blake ever did.

Blake is in the past.

My three guys, though, they are my future, and I won't give them up for anything. They make me feel alive and push me past my limits, which is exactly what I wanted, what I craved when I first started college.

I wanted to explore this *thing* inside me, without feeling ashamed, like I did with Blake.

I am finding myself. Discovering exactly who I am sexually, and okay, so it might be unconventional, but I'm not broken. I'm not something that needs to be fixed and stuffed in a box like my ex wanted. I can't be someone I'm not.

My guys ruin me in all the right ways, and they are there to help me pick up the pieces of myself once they are done. I've never felt so... *desired*, and it makes me feel powerful.

"As much as I'd like to, I can't, Savannah. I have this thing that I have to do tonight, and I can't get out of it, you know that," River says, drawing me from my thoughts. *Oh yeah, I asked a question.* I pout, giving my best friend my most adorable puppy dog eyes.

"Don't make me face my stepbrothers and parents alone, *please*." I make praying hands and bat my lashes at her. I have plenty more where this comes from.

River sighs and shakes her head, but the broken look in her eyes gives me pause.

Has something happened?

She's been acting weird for the past two weeks, and she's never around much anymore. She looks exhausted, and I wonder if she's been sleeping. I notice that her face is a little drawn, as if she's lost a little weight. I'm worried about her.

"Savannah, they are your stepbrothers, and

Jackson is basically your family. You will be fine. Besides, your mom will be there." Her curt tone irritates me because she's not usually so dismissive. I think better than to say anything, because it's clear that something is bothering her. I have tried to get her to open up about it, but she just changes the subject. The closest thing to her breaking down the walls she's been building these past couple of weeks was when she told me, *'My past is biting me in the ass.'* All I can do is be there for her and let her know that I'm not going anywhere, no matter what. She'll tell me when she's ready, and if she's not, that's okay.

"Fine. I have to get dressed," I mutter, trying to mask my worry. If I pry too much, she'll shut down for good, I just know it.

"What's the big deal? What happened to you finding them hot and wanting to take a wild ride on their disco sticks or whatever it was you used to say?"

Oh my God. I totally forgot about that. This is what happens when you've known someone for a long time. They remember all of your embarrassing, not-so-bright moments.

Turning around, I pull my shirt over my head, and keep my back to her so she can't see my cheeks tinge red.

"I never meant it," I lie, and internally wince at how unconvincing I sound.

"Ah, I call bullshit." I fight not to cringe as I quickly change, then turn around to face her.

"Nope. Not anymore. I don't find them attractive the way I u—"

"Swear on my life, Savannah Carter. Swear that you have never pictured their faces as you made yourself come?"

Fuck.

This time, I do cringe, and hate that she's right. She knows me too well. The smug look on her face tells me that she sees right through my crap, and instead of saying anything more on the topic, I storm out of my room, muttering about how much I hate her. Her laughter follows after me, and I smile, knowing she can't see me do so. I hope she's a little happier than she was before. God knows she looks like she needs the distraction.

Her words play on repeat in my head, and she's right. I've pictured their faces hundreds of times, and I carry out those fantasies through the three tall strangers in masks, wishing it were them instead.

I roll to a stop in front of my mom and stepfather's mansion, and I look over to see that Kale's car is already here. I hate that they arrived before me. It would have been better if I were the one who got here first, so I didn't have to face them right away. Nerves rear their ugly head, building in the pit of my stomach, because now I can't avoid talking to them like I had hoped.

"Stop being a fucking pussy, Savannah. You've been fucking three complete strangers with hidden faces for weeks, and you can't even face your stepbrothers, and Jackson? Get it together, girl," I scold myself before climbing out of the car, putting one foot in front of the other. I keep my head held high as I walk through the front door, take off my coat and hang it on the coat rack. Chatter sounds from the dining room, and I give myself a pep talk to go in there. Before I lose my nerve, I rip the proverbial band-aid off and head on in, reminding myself that I don't need their approval.

I tell myself that they mean nothing to me. Shit would be a whole lot less complicated if that were actually true.

I am a grown ass woman. I have not one, not two, but three hot as fuck men who want me. I have no business crushing on my stepbrothers, and I sure as hell have no business crushing on Jackson, either, not after everything with my guys.

"Savannah!" My mom's voice breaks over the chatter as I walk past the threshold and into the dining room where everyone is seated. I deserve an Oscar with how good this fake ass smile plastered on my face is.

Within seconds, I can feel all three of their gazes on me, burning my skin like their eyes are made of hellfire. I try my absolute best to ignore them as I round the table to hug my mom.

She smells like jasmine and *home,* and God, I miss her. I hate that she and I have drifted apart since she married my stepfather, Kalvin.

He hasn't done anything wrong to me, but the way he has treated his sons growing up has never sat right with me. Nothing Reign nor Kale do is ever good enough for him, and he has always looked down his nose at Jackson, despite him basically growing up here. He's a hard man, but he's even harder to fucking please, and I suppose I just feel like they deserve better.

I release my mom and turn to face Kalvin, greeting him with a nod. He grunts, as per his usual, and I grit my teeth to keep from calling his arrogant ass out for it. I run my gaze over the table, and my stomach sinks when I see that the only available seat is between Kale and Jackson, because, of course, it is.

When I lock eyes with Kale, the *sonofabitch* smirks. His dark hair falls just above his eyes, and I curse myself for how my pussy throbs in response. I would flip him the bird, but my parents are present and I'd rather not start shit this early in the evening. He's wearing a black Henley, and it only hugs his defined, solid body. I can't ignore the way his muscles flex, and when I look up, I realize that he's noticed me staring. He bites his bottom lip, rolling his smoldering eyes over my body before coming back up to meet my eyes.

I swear I can feel the heat radiating off him. I stalk around the table, saying nothing, as I pull out my chair and take a seat, making a conscious effort not to brush against the guys at my sides.

The sound of Jackson's low laugh only pisses me off. I know they know that I'm ignoring them on purpose, but I feign nonchalance and focus on my mom.

"So, how's school? How are your classes going?" Mom questions, and I launch into a spiel that I practiced on the way over, avoiding almost everything, and only telling her about the classes I am excelling in. The last thing I want is for Kalvin to know that I failed two classes this semester. I'd never hear the fucking end of it, and it would only ruin this dinner for my mother.

"Well, at least you're actually learning something considering the amount we pay for all three of your tuition," Kalvin interjects, and my body grows rigid, knowing that was more of a dig at his sons than it was at me. I bet Jackson's thanking his lucky stars he got a full ride, because it's one less thing Kalvin has over his head.

"It pains us to constantly disappoint you, Pops. We swear to never act up again, and live like angels for the rest of our lives," Reign says in a sarcastic tone. He's everything dangerous and tempting as his dark, unruly hair falls into his face. It's perfectly messy, and the number of times I've imagined running my fingers through it is embarrassing, because it's a lot.

Kalvin shoots him a glare and opens his mouth to argue, but Mom places a hand on his arm, smiling up at him warmly. "Can you help me serve up supper, dear?" Kalvin shoots his sons a glare before following Mom out of the room. I'm unable to keep up the act any longer and slouch in my chair with a sigh.

"Savy, baby," Reign purrs, and I loll my head to the side and quirk a brow at him.

Okay, Savy, baby? *Really?* He's still going to call me that?

"It's Savannah."

His dark eyes don't leave mine as he just sits there, his masculine presence commanding the room. I say nothing, and the low chuckle that rumbles from his lips has me focusing on Jax instead. I refuse to buy into their banter tonight.

"You look good, baby," Jax says, and I choose to ignore the way heat creeps up my body at his compliment. Jackson is the kind of man everyone stares at. He's tall, taller than the twins by maybe an inch, but it's his eyes that have everyone weak in the knees. They're the most beautiful green I think I have ever seen. There are a few guys with green eyes in my classes, but they've got nothing on Jax.

"Can we all just agree to have *somewhat* of a normal dinner? I'm not in the mood for your games, okay?" I utter, and a gasp escapes me when Kale's hand lands on my thigh. My breath hitches, and my every thought is robbed. The only thing I can focus on is his large hand on my body, and the lustful look gleaming in his eyes.

"No games, baby. Just the truth." This comes from Kale, making my brows knit in confusion as I try to decipher what the hell he's talking about.

"Truth about what?"

"Us," Reign answers, and lava flows through my veins as Kale slides his hand higher and higher up under my skirt, until I feel his pinky finger brush against my pussy.

Oh my God.

I jolt upright in my chair, heart lurching in my chest, just as my mom and Kalvin's voices bring me back to reality, and they enter the room, carrying trays of food.

I can't think.

I can barely breathe because Kale Jagger's hand is touching me, and my traitorous pussy is pulsing. I've been fucked every night for weeks, and yet the feeling of Kale on my sensitive flesh has me hungrier than I have ever been, and I don't mean for food.

As Mom and Kalvin reclaim their seats, I let out a soft, involuntary gasp when Jax boldly places his hand on my other thigh. Heat surges through me as Kale and Jax's fingers interlock, purposefully brushing their hands against my throbbing pussy. I can't suppress the agonizing sigh that escapes my lips.

Mom casts a worried glance, her brows pulling together in a frown.

"Savannah, honey, are you okay?" she asks, her voice filled with genuine care for me.

"Y-yeah, why?" I squeak.

"You look flushed, sweetheart. Are you coming down with something?" Her concern is sweet, but if she knew the reason why I look this way, she'd be clutching her pearls like a rosary, praying to God to save her sweet daughter.

There's no saving a girl like me.

"Yeah, Savy, are you *coming* down with something? You look so flustered." Reign's innuendo is clear, and the vicious smirk on his handsome fucking face makes my fingers twitch with the urge to smack him.

"I'm peachy." The words drip from my mouth, but they sound more like a threat. All three of these assholes snort a laugh, and they begin to pile their plates with food. They're acting like nothing happened, but I'm too wound up to even consider eating.

Dinner seemed to drag on, and the entire time, Jax and Kale capitalized on my sitting between them. They've been brushing against me all night, placing their hands on me like they own every inch. I smacked them away without drawing attention, because if anyone knew what they were doing, shit would well and truly hit the fucking fan.

I'd be a liar if I said I didn't love the feeling of their hands on me, and I know that I shouldn't, but I can't fucking help it.

Once dinner is over, we retire to the living room. I chose the seat furthest from everybody, but Jax and Kale only followed. Mom and Kalvin have disappeared into the kitchen to make coffee, and I'm thinking that maybe I should join them. You could cut the sexual tension in this room with a knife, and if it's obvious to me, it'll be obvious to our parents.

When I go to stand, Kale places his hand on my thigh, pinning me to my seat. My head whips to the side to face him, and his knowing expression has my heart pumping loudly in my ears.

He says nothing as he slides his hand up under my skirt again, only this time, he cups my pussy, dripping with need. I launch out of my chair, just as Mom and Kalvin return, and everyone's attention is on me.

"I need to use the bathroom. Excuse me," I mutter as I walk across the room and down the hall. I bypass the downstairs bathroom, then climb the stairs to the second level. I need to create as much distance between me and that room as possible.

I slam the door closed, then lock it behind me.

What the fuck was that?

I've always been attracted to the three of them, and I'm not an idiot. I know that they're attracted to me too, but they've never acted on it until now. Why?

"Pull it together. They're just messing with you," I hiss, staring at my flushed complexion in the mirror. I splash water on my face to cool off and attempt to calm my racing heart. Usually, I act unaffected by them, though they don't *usually* play with my pussy at the dinner table, with our parents less than three feet away, either.

They destroyed my panties, they are completely soaked.

I don't even know how to process what just happened, so I take another minute to gather myself before stepping out of the bathroom. I have every intention of heading straight back downstairs, but as I pass by Kale's old room, I notice that the door is slightly ajar.

Curiosity gets the better of me, and I'm suddenly moving forward until I'm standing in the doorway. The door creaks as I nudge it open further, and my gaze sweeps the room. It's exactly like I remember it when we were growing up. Band posters are hung haphazardly on the walls, and I smile because that's how we first bonded all those years ago. We share the same taste in music, and nostalgia has me walking around, relishing in memory lane, but I spot his duffle bag on the bed with the top unzipped.

I shouldn't.

Don't do it, Savannah.

"Fuck it," I mutter to myself, fingers prying the flap open, then I reel back with a gasp, fury and disbelief crashing through me at what's sitting on top.

No way.

I've always hated being in Kalvin's presence.

The bastard never passes up the chance to throw shade at the twins or call them useless. He always makes them feel like a complete fucking waste of his money, and because he's paying for them to go to college, they never hear the end of it.

He's a piece of shit.

The only reason Kale and Reign even bother attending these bullshit dinners is to spare Savannah from facing him alone. If it were up to them, they would never see their father again, and I wouldn't blame them for cutting all ties. They figure that if their dad is taking his mood swings out on them, he's leaving her alone, and nothing matters more to them than her.

She's everything to us, and she always will be.

"Are you failing your classes? Have you decided to grow fucking brains? Or am I wasting my breath, time, and money on your tuition, like everything else?" the fucker asks smugly, as he swirls his whiskey in his hand. He doesn't even bother to look at them when he speaks, and I clench my glass hard until my knuckles turn white.

I'm surprised that it doesn't break.

I bite the inside of my cheek to shut my fucking mouth, because I am sick of it. I've been watching this shit for years, and because they took me in, I've never dared say anything for fear of losing the twins. I'd rather die than let that happen. But each time we sit here, it gets harder and harder for me to stay silent.

"You can cut us off anytime you want, Fath—" Before Kale can finish, Savannah storms into the room like a fucking hurricane. My brows knit in confusion, but before I can question if she is okay, she throws Kale's duffle bag on the floor at her feet, then takes a seat on the couch opposite us.

Kalvin and Karina begin their usual sermon, criticizing her friend River and suggesting she should associate with a more *polished* group, however, their words are completely ignored as her gaze remains fixed on the three of us.

If looks could burn you alive, we'd be nothing more than ash and embers.

Anxiety crawls its way up my spine before settling in the pit of my stomach, because I think that she's pissed with us. Either that, or maybe something happened.

Kale's eyes are fixated on his bag, and I put two and two together. Whatever she's found in there isn't good.

Reign must have had the same thoughts as I had, and rises to his feet, snatching up the bag, and when his face blanks and his shoulders hunch, everything around me stills.

His eyes meet Savannah's, and I know that shit is about to hit the fan.

"Was this a game to you three?" she spits out, her eyes welling with tears, and I don't miss it when her voice cracks. Seeing her like this, looking at us like we've betrayed her, spears me right in the fucking chest.

Kale and I both stand, and so does she, and I can feel her pulling away from us. Reign doesn't move, the duffle bag forgotten as he gazes down at her pleadingly. The look on his face is one I've never seen him wear before.

He's in pain.

The thought of losing her right now is too fucking much, and the love of my life, my best friend, is hurting.

I reach for her, but she backs up a step, shaking her head, dismissing me. She wipes away the tears now falling down her face, and I feel like my knees could give out at any moment. I'm one fucking sob away from begging her to stay with us. Begging for her to give us a moment to explain things.

I can't believe this is happening.

She knows that the strangers behind the masks are us, and it fucking breaks something inside me that she found out this way in front of her parents.

"You were so much more than a game to us, Savannah. You were always the prize," Kale says, his voice breaking as the weight of this moment sinks in. We never meant to hurt her, and we especially didn't mean to deceive her.

"What the hell is going on here?" Kalvin snaps, but we all ignore him. Now is not the time for him to pretend like he gives a fuck about any of us. He only cares about how we make him look, and while that used to matter to me, I am theirs, not his, and they need me right now.

"You fucking lied to me! You used me and... *you tricked me.*" My chest cracks when tears begin to roll down her cheeks. We didn't mean to betray her trust, and I can't fucking stand the way she is looking at us. Worse than she ever looked at Blake.

"It was the only way—"

"Shut up!" she screams, cutting Reign off before he can even finish. "You could have told me. At any time, you could have told me that you were them. But you made me believe you were..."

"Someone else?" Kale says, his tone short and dejected. He steps around me and stops a foot away from her to stand with Reign. Kale gazes down at our girl, his heart in his throat. "You can lie to the fucking world, baby, but you can't lie to us."

"*Baby?*" Kalvin hisses, but no one pays him or Savannah's mother any attention.

"You wanted it to be us. You wanted us, Savy, but you were too afraid to come and get us. The truth is, we wanted you, too. Always have, and always will, and we've spent years waiting for the right time to make you ours. Don't let this be the end, Little Viper." The pained look on Reign's face is unfamiliar to me, and my heart breaks at how cut open and raw he is. This is a first, and since being with our girl, he's grown more open with his feelings. The sad part about leaving yourself open like this is you're vulnerable to getting hurt, and I worry that if this goes bad, he'll never let anybody in again, and I don't know what that will mean for the three of us.

For him and me.

"The worst part isn't even the fact that you all lied to me, it's that I mattered so little to you all that you thought I deserved the lie in the first place."

Suddenly, I think I get it.

Grief.

She's grieving the loss of the three faceless men, because they weren't just characters in a stupid fucking game to her. They were real. And by finding out that it was actually us behind them, she feels like she's lost them forever.

It's written all over her face.

She feels betrayed because we made her fall in love with men that no longer exist, and she found out in the worst possible way imaginable.

"You haven't lost us, baby. We were always *us* beneath those masks. But, baby, there isn't a single reality where we don't end up together, and you know it. We know you, the real you, and we were always yours. No matter where we are, who we are, or what we're doing, you're buried so deep under our skin that you've rewired our fucking veins, baby. *Fuck,* we were yours from the moment you first stepped foot in this house, and you're ours now, Savannah." My throat is hoarse, torn open by the weight of the words I just let fall from my lips. But it's the truth, and that's all I can give her.

"Someone better start fucking explaining what the hell is going on here before I lose my cool completely," Kalvin roars, and all our gazes finally fall to him. He's insignificant in all of this, and whatever happens next, I'm not so sure any of us cares. Our only focus and concern right now is Savannah, and how she's handling this whole situation. We need her to try to understand where we are coming from, otherwise we risk losing her forever.

Savy turns and faces Kalvin, focusing the brunt of her anger on him.

Thank the Lord for small miracles.

I tense, knowing that shit is about to pop off when he learns the truth about what we have been doing with his precious stepdaughter. He may not care about his sons, but he has shown that Savannah is the one he puts on a pedestal. Yet, the twins and I have never held that against her.

"I've sort of been in a relationship with three

guys, and I had no idea that those guys were *your* sons and Jackson. It's a long story." Never one to mince words or lie, Savannah just comes right out with it, and I didn't expect the sudden relief I feel that everything is out in the open.

Kalvin's face immediately transforms, and I notice the second her words sink in, and he finally registers what everything means. He slowly turns to the three of us with nothing but disgust and *hatred* in his eyes.

"I always knew you two were already disappointments, but I never expected that you would drag her down with your fucked-up bullshit!" he roars, pointing his index finger in my direction. Savannah and her mom flinch, but neither of them says anything as Reign, Kale, and I stand a little taller beneath his gaze, brimming with contempt.

"Sir, I can explain," I say, my voice calmer than I feel, but he shuts me down, spinning around on his heels, and smashes his glass of whiskey at the wall behind Savannah and Karina. We all stand stock still, my eyes on Savannah and her mom as they sit there, wide-eyed, shocked at how close he was to hitting them. Kale's golden eyes go dark as he stares at his father, while Reign rushes over to comfort our girl and her mother. Karina is sobbing, her shoulders are slumped as she shakes in Savannah's arms, and I fucking hate myself for it.

It was not supposed to end up like this.

Karina is a good person, and she's way too fucking good for Kalvin Jagger. This isn't the first time he's acted out like this, but usually the twins are on the receiving end. However, there have been more than a few times when he has hit Karina whenever she's come to our defense over the years. Now she says almost nothing at all. I used to think that Karina and Savannah were basically the same person, only her mom was much older. Yet, as time goes by, the light in her eyes has dulled, and she's a shell of the person she used to be.

That's the kind of man he is.

He takes beautiful and happy things and molds them into whatever he wants, fitting his vision for himself and his image. And when he realizes he can't mold or change you, he breaks you and changes how everybody sees you instead.

Kale steps forward, standing an inch away from his father's face. I step up beside him, because if Kalvin fucking Jagger touches a single hair on my boy's head, he'll be eating from a fucking straw for the next month.

"You're upset, so I'm gonna let the fact that you

just put our girl and her mother in danger slide. I can't speak for the others. I want to make something abundantly clear, Father." Kale spits the word *father* like it's acid on his tongue, before he continues. "We don't give a single flying rat's sweaty fucking asshole what you think of us. We don't even give a shit about your money. Correction, our mother's money. But you can take it all away right fucking now, and we wouldn't stop you. The only reason, and I fucking mean it when I say *the only reason,* we stuck around here after Mom died, was because of that girl who walked through our door no more than a week after losing our mother." I reach out and brush a gentle stroke along Kale's exposed skin of his neck, and he must come back down to earth, because his shoulders loosen, and he almost pushes into my touch.

Reign stands at his brother's other side, staring daggers at his father.

"We love her, Dad. She makes us happy, and I know that you like to destroy the things that make us happy, but for that to happen, you'd be destroying yourself. Because you have nothing to gain and everything to lose if you don't play this right," Reign says, his voice surprisingly even, and I know it's only to calm his brother down.

We have seen what Kale is capable of if push

comes to shove, and we don't want to make this something it doesn't need to be if we can help it.

"Do you think I give a fuck about what you three think love is? You haven't lived long enough to know how to fucking spell it, let alone feel it. All you boys ever do is screw and screw and screw until everything is completely fucked. Well, you've fucked the wrong whore this time. She's your stepsister. You can't be together. And I don't know what sick, and twisted fucking games you've been playing with her, but it ends tonight. Pack your shit."

Kale tenses beneath my touch, and Reign's eyes glaze over with something unrecognizable as they stare at their father. Kalvin's face is red with anger, and I know there's nothing I can do or say that will hold him back.

"Call her a fucking whore again, I fucking dare you," Reign growls, his tone not one to be fucked with.

"We're not leaving without her," Kale says, his voice calmer than his twin's, which only makes him sound scarier.

"She's not going anywhere with you. Get your shit and get out!"

"My daughter is not a whore," a hesitant voice chimes in from our side, a little fragile and uncertain.

All our eyes turn to see Karina, staring at her husband like she'd much rather watch paint dry.

"Mom, it's fine–"

"No, Savannah. It isn't fine. I am tired, Kalvin. I am tired of sitting on the sidelines watching you destroy our son's lives, and subsequently, your own, because you are so filled with hatred and vitriol that you can't recognize how good they truly are. They are star players, and you refuse to watch a single game of theirs. Your excuse? Football is nothing more than a glorified hobby. And Savannah, my baby girl, she is bright, witty, and such a talented artist that I know one day we'll be seeing her work all over the world."

"Mom," Savannah chokes, a mix of emotions rising to the surface at the pride in her mother's voice.

"My daughter is not a whore, and you should be ashamed of yourself."

"I'll say whatever the damn hell I like in my own fucking house, Karina. Were you not listening? Savannah has been fucking them, all three of them, and my sons might be fucked up, but none of this would have happened if your daughter didn't fuck everything that moves!"

There's a second of silence before Reign slams

his fist into his father's jaw, so hard his head snaps sideways. Kalvin stumbles backward and falls to the polished marble floor. Blood spills from his nose and mouth, and the shrill sounds of stressful cries and panic fill the room.

Kale doesn't hold his brother back as he delivers two more hits, even harder than the first punch, as well as a heavy booted kick to his ribs. Kale doesn't spare his father a single glance before he reaches out and places a steadying hand on Reign's shoulder.

Kalvin just laughs a low, maniacal laugh, spitting blood to the floor as he staggers to his feet.

"If you aren't out by the time I get back, I'll have all, and I mean all your sorry asses thrown in jail for trespassing," he says through clenched teeth, his eyes flicking to Karina, then back to us, shaking his head in disdain.

Without another word, he shoulder-checks me as he walks past, grabs his keys from the sideboard, then leaves through the front door, breaking his wife's heart into thousands of tiny irreparable pieces as he leaves.

THIRTEEN
REIGN

There are times in life when you experience loss. And when you lose someone you love, it feels like the air has been ripped from your lungs, and you're left behind to slowly suffocate to death.

That's what it felt like earlier when we almost lost our girl.

And then there are other times when loss feels like a blessing. A strange kind of relief that rids your life of all that was old and rotten, to make way for something better and new.

But when the police officer stood at my door, informing my brother and me that just two hours before our father had been killed in a hit-and-run, it didn't make me feel anything at all. There was no sadness, no pain, or despair for the man who gave me and my brother life, as I stood back watching our Savannah cradle her mother in her arms, while Kale, Jackson, and I thanked the officer and closed the door.

It was a long night of back-and-forth questioning with the police, as they investigated whether we could think of anyone who might have held a grudge against Kalvin. Unless they were prepared to write the names of every person he'd ever been associated with in their little black notebook, they were wasting their time.

Kale took Karina down to the coroner's office to identify his body, and when they returned, they all went in separate directions. Kale went straight to his bedroom, and Karina and Savannah bunked together in Savannah's room because Karina couldn't bring herself to sleep in the bed she and Kalvin shared. Not just because he died, but because of how they left things when he walked out on her earlier.

We all tried to tell Karina that he wasn't thinking straight, that he didn't mean what he said to her, but she knew that he did. She also knew that her little outburst in our defense was going to cost her when he got home, and there isn't a single doubt in my mind that he would have hurt her. Now that he's dead, he'll never hurt her again.

Savannah hasn't spoken a word to any of us or even looked in our direction. It would make this night a whole lot better if she'd just forgive us and move on. But she's with her mom, and she needs her right now.

And then there's me. Lying here in my bed, staring up at the ceiling—it isn't helping me shut my fucking mind off. All I can think about is how our Little Viper feels in my arms, how sweet she tastes, and the sounds she makes when she's about to come.

I think I lost that tonight, and the hole in my chest put there by the mere thought of her no longer being ours has me all up in my head. I never meant for any of this to happen. I never meant for her to feel like we had betrayed her, and I sure as fuck didn't mean for her to feel like she lost us the minute our identities were revealed.

A knock sounds at my door, and my heart skips a beat, hoping it's my baby girl, but when the door opens, the hallway light that trickles in is bright enough for me to make out who it is. I slump back against my pillows, equal parts thankful that he came, and wishing he didn't have to see me like this. All strung out and fucking depressed at this whole situation with Savy.

"Fuck, okay. Tell me that you wish it were

someone else standing here, without telling me." Jax's dry ass joke does nothing, and I know he's only trying to make me laugh. He usually always does, but I just don't have it in me tonight. With a sigh, he walks in, leaving the door slightly ajar, and sits on the edge of the bed, staring down at me.

"I know that you and Kale hated him, but he was still your father," he says quietly, his voice soft and comforting.

I scrub a hand down my face and grumble in frustration.

"I don't even care that he's dead," I admit. I feel like a piece of shit for feeling nothing, but I just don't. Call it shock or whatever, but I just don't.

"A part of you does care, but it's buried beneath all the pain and PTSD."

I shake my head. "I feel numb, and all I can think about is how we fucked up. Savy has pulled so far away from us, and I can't guarantee that we'll ever get her back."

"She's ours, Reign. She may not be ready to admit that shit yet, but she will be soon once she processes everything. We are never letting her go. She knows this."

"Jackson, has it ever occurred to you that now Kalvin is dead, she's no longer tied to us? Have you thought about the fact that she never has to set foot in this house again if she doesn't want to? Her pin won't mark this house on the map anymore if her mother leaves, and sure, we could follow her around like shadows, but the tie that pulled us together is disintegrating as each minute passes that she's not here with us." I clear the lump in my throat and look away, hating that I feel so fucking helpless when it comes to Savannah.

"Baby," Jax says softly. He raises his hand and slowly glides his fingertips across my cheek. "You're thinking too many thoughts at once. Let's just focus on what we can control. Stay here in the now with me. As long as we have each other, we can handle anything. I know the thought of losing her is gut-wrenching, but you've always got me, love." His fingers catch the tear I didn't even know was falling down my cheek.

His thumb pauses at the corner of my mouth, then traces a slow line across my lips. When he reaches my bottom lip, he presses on it just enough to pull it down. "You have no idea what you do to me, Reign Jagger." His low voice pierces me right through the chest, and it hits me that I don't think I could survive in a world without Jackson Graves in it.

"Losing her would be the greatest tragedy, Jax. But losing you would be soul-destroying." That's all I get to say before his mouth is on mine. My heart pounds loudly in my ears as my every nerve awakens with the taste of his mouth. His tongue tangles with mine as we lean into each other, desperate to feel every broken piece of us.

His hands reach out to tug off my shirt, and our lips reluctantly part as we throw it to the floor. His hands are immediately on my body, as he looms over me, trailing kisses along my jawline, then along my neck, before hovering over my ear.

"I want you, baby."

"Then have me. Until the day you realize I'm no good for you... I'm yours. Always." His mouth is back on mine in an instant, then he quickly pulls away as he pushes me back against my pillow. He looms over me, the hallway light highlighting the contours of his delectable body. I reach out and trace the matching ink the three of us share, etched across his heart.

Ever thine, ever mine, ever ours.

We will always belong to him, my brother and I, and he will always belong to us.

Together forever, with no exit.

A vow that only we understand.

I curse myself for thinking that Savannah understood too. Well, I think that maybe she does, it's just fucking complicated.

The door slowly creaks open, and more light spills into the room as my brother stands in the doorway. We break our gaze to look over at Kale, who just stands there, silently watching us for a beat. I quirk a brow, as if to silently ask if he's joining us, then he walks past the threshold and closes the door behind him.

His footsteps fill the quiet room as he walks over to the window and pulls back the curtains. Moonlight filters in, illuminating my bedroom and casting shadows over Jackson's body, still above me.

"Got room for one more?" Kale says sheepishly, standing at the foot of my bed.

"Get over here," Jackson says with a quiet, breathy chuckle, and he climbs off the bed to be with Kale. I instantly miss his warmth, so I sit up a little, pulling back the blankets to make it easier for us to climb under. I lean with my back pressed against my headboard and wait for them. Kale looks rigid and closed off, but when Jax pulls him into his arms to comfort him, his shoulders loosen.

I haven't had a moment to talk with him about tonight, but I know my twin better than anyone. He's heartbroken.

I watch as their silhouettes move together in a feverish kiss, whispering in each other's ears before Jax places his hands on either side of Kale's bare shoulders, then guides him to the bed beside me.

"Take your pants off," he demands, and a smile teases the corner of my lips because I know that he's about to unleash his depraved inner self on us. Kale raises a brow, and he smiles a knowing smile before letting out a soft laugh. Standing, he does as Jax says, and I take this moment to revel in the man before me, taking control of his guys.

This never happens.

He never takes control in the bedroom, not before Savannah, and not since that time in the woods when we first claimed her. I won't deny that the thought of him owning and claiming me in every way imaginable makes my *fully alert* cock twitch with need and anticipation.

"You, too, Reign. Strip."

I bite the inside of my mouth to prevent myself from smiling, just in case he feels like denying me what I think is coming as a form of punishment. I climb to my knees and slowly pull my boxers down over my hips. Jax's eyes are fixated on my movements, biting his bottom lip as my dick springs out, slapping my abs. Once my pants are off, I toss them at him, and he growls.

"*Watch it,*" he spits, and holy fucking shit, he's not playing.

"You better behave yourself, brother, because I'm not sure we can handle whoever the fuck took over Jackson's body just now," Kale says, his voice teasing, and Jax is standing in front of his face in a split second.

"Get on your knees, you mouthy cunt, and suck my fucking cock."

Death.

I have experienced death at some point in the past two minutes, because this version of Jackson is fucking heaven.

I must make some sort of sound, because the look he shoots me isn't one I've ever seen before.

"Don't think you're getting out of this, on your fucking knees, Reign." *Wait. What?* "Did I fucking stutter, Jagger? *On. Your. Fucking. Knees.*" I don't think I've moved so fast in my life. I do as he says, kneeling beside my brother as Jax's cock hovers above us. Kale looks nervously at me before quickly turning back to face Jax. "Open your mouth," Jax demands, rubbing the tip of his swollen cock along my lips. I part them, and he shoves his cock so deep into my mouth that I almost forget how to breathe. I relax my throat, and as I do, he reaches out and abruptly fists my hair, then starts slowly thrusting his thick cock in and out of my mouth.

"Fuck, baby. Your hot mouth feels so fucking good on my cock." My own dick twitches at the sound of his praise, and when my throat makes that infamous gluck gluck sound, he hangs his head back and moans. Loud. "Kale?"

"Yes, Jackson," Kale answers like the fucking teacher's pet that he is.

"I want to feel your mouth on my balls, baby." Without hesitation, Kale takes Jackson's heavy balls into his mouth one at a time, sucking and licking them, and Jax's moans fill the room as we take him closer and closer to the edge. "Fuck! Yes, just like that. *Ugh.* I love it when you're both on your knees for me. Feasting on my cock like a bunch of starving fucking whores." His deep voice rolls off me, and it only sends blood straight to my weeping dick. He thrusts into my mouth harder, my eyes watery, my saliva fucking everywhere, but before we can make him come, he rips my head back by my hair and removes his length from my mouth. He takes a few steps back, and Kale and I spare each other a confused glance. We rise to our feet and step in closer to him, not knowing what's next.

"Reign, I want you to fuck my throat while Kale baby fucks my ass."

Halle-fucking-lujah.

I watch as their shadows move together in the moonlight, their touches desperate and possessive, and Kale's hand rises to fist Jax's hair, guiding his mouth to his in an urgent kiss. Their tongues tangle as they breathe each other in, and I lean into the side of Jackson's neck, leaving a slow trail of soft, lingering kisses behind before sucking his earlobe into my mouth. I gently sink my teeth into it, and he fucking purrs, still kissing my brother as my hot breath teases the sensitive skin on his neck.

I look down to see that Kale is slowly beating and squeezing our lover's cock, and the world narrows when Jackson reaches for mine, wrapping his large hand around it until it throbs almost painfully in his hold.

I fucking need more.

My head is clouded with desire as he slowly pumps my cock from base to tip, and when his fingers start circling the pre-cum leaking from my swollen tip, he turns fucking feral.

He pumps me harder and harder as Kale bites

Jackson's bottom lip, kissing him deeper as our desperate panting fills the room around us. I lean away abruptly, causing Jax to release my dick from his hold, and he whines in frustration.

I need his fucking mouth.

Understanding flashes across his face, and he shoves Kale away, who reluctantly obeys. Jackson's green eyes are darker than I have ever seen them as they bounce between my twin and me, standing at his mercy before him as we wait for his next move.

"If I don't have you now, I'm going to lose my ever-loving mind," Kale rasps, and Jax focuses his gaze on him.

"Then have me, Kale. I'm all yours, baby. Fuck me like you own me, love." In an instant, Kale moves to stand behind Jax, and the wide, excited grin on my brother's face is noticeable, even in the dark. I move in closer when Kale grips Jackson's shoulder with one hand, signaling him to bend over, the whole time Jax's eyes never leaving mine.

"I love it when you're like this. Bent over with my hard cock in your face. You look like a fucking dream, Jackson," I say, my voice barely above a whisper as Kale spits into his hand.

"I'm gonna fuck you so good, Jax. I'm gonna fill

your tight ass with my cock until you're begging for my cum."

"Yes. I want you so bad, Kale," Jax breathes, his mouth opening on a whimper as Kale prepares Jax's hole for his dick.

"You're ours, Jackson. Ours to hold. Ours to fuck. Ours to own. There is no fucking way out, baby."

"No way out," he replies, and my cock throbs when his warm breath hits my skin. Kale doesn't waste any more time before sliding into him. I grip Jax's hair at the same time, and his mouth immediately wraps around my hard dick. His hands reach out to grip my hips, and with each hard thrust from Kale, Jax takes my cock deeper and deeper into his mouth. His fingers dig into my flesh as he sucks me, my cock pulsing in his mouth with each movement against his wet tongue.

"Fuck! You're so fucking tight, baby. Your hole is fucking swallowing my dick!" Kale murmurs, his voice raw and ragged, straining as he relishes in the pleasure we're giving each other.

"You like being used by us, don't you, Jax? You love it when we fuck you hard, filling you with our cum at both ends." He sobs as I fuck his mouth harder, and the vibration from his blissful cries only fuels the intense pleasure burning through me.

The sound of skin slapping against skin bounces off the walls around us, and it's almost enough to have me tumbling over the edge. We drown in the heat, as our bodies become one, lost in the intoxicating rapture of euphoria and ecstasy that's consuming us whole.

"You suck me so good, Jax. Your hot, greedy mouth was fucking made for devouring my cock." I don't even know what I'm saying as my heavy balls tighten, begging for release. Kale growls, his thrusts growing even more frantic as he gets closer and closer to his breaking point. Jackson's tongue flattens, and he relaxes his throat, making way for my cock as he takes all of me in.

"I'm gonna fucking come for you, Jax!" Kale cries, and Jackson whimpers around my dick in response. Kale pumps three more times before he plummets, surrendering to the pleasure in the way that only Jackson can give him. Kale's body falls limply, covering Jackson's back, completely sated and blissed out.

I thrust into Jax's mouth like I'm fucking starving for him, because I fucking am. My cock hits the back of his throat before I finally come undone. My eyes squeeze shut as I dive completely into the ecstasy washing like violent waves over me, before I open them to see Jackson staring up at me like I am everything he's been praying for.

I'm still for a moment as Kale pulls out of Jackson with a jerk, and when Jackson straightens, he brings his mouth up to meet mine in a transcendental kiss, and my cum that fills his mouth suddenly fills mine, as our tongues twist, curling around each other, until we both swallow my release.

"That's so fucking hot, Reign." His voice is rough from being throat fucked, and I let out a breathy chuckle, shaking my head at how depraved he is beneath his polished scholarship football persona everyone admires. But they have no idea just how fucking dirty he gets for my twin and me.

"I want you to eat me," he says, and my heart skips a fucking beat. "I want you both to eat me." Without another word, he walks over to the bed and lies down on the mattress, looking back at us as if to tell us to hurry our asses up. Kale raises a brow before shrugging, then walks over to where our lover lies waiting for us. I follow, not caring in the slightest how fucking taboo this is.

This is us.

This is how we are together, and I wouldn't have it any other way.

Jackson raises his legs and rests them on both our

shoulders, as my twin and I hover before Jackson's thoroughly fucked ass. I place a hand on the back of Jackson's thigh, pushing his leg back even further so we can both get a better look at how good his fucking hole looks in the glow of the moon, dripping with my brother's cum.

Kale's tongue darts out and licks along the edge of his hole, tasting his own release. I immediately follow behind him. Licking and sucking the cum from Jackson's sensitive flesh, before sticking my tongue as deep as I can inside him.

"*Ah–fuck!* That feels so fucking good!" he mewls. Kale presses his mouth to the spot between Jax's cock and his asshole, and it only makes him shudder from the sheer pleasure that both our tongues are giving him.

"Do you like that, baby? Do you like it when my twin's tongue fucks your ass?" Kale teases before diving back in to lick his skin clean.

"I do. I fucking love it. I don't think I'll ever get enough of you both."

We lie awake for what feels like hours, our bodies

tangled and content like this in the dark. Kale's hand is in Jackson's hair, stroking him tenderly.

"Jax?" I whisper, not sure if he's awake or not. When he hums into the crook of my neck, I know that he's caught somewhere in the space between consciousness and sleep.

"I love you."

His breath hitches, and he rises, using his elbows for support as he stares down at me in utter disbelief.

I've never said those words before.

Not to him.

I know he knows I love him, but I've never said it out loud until now. With everything that's happened tonight, knowing that we may have lost the love of all our lives has done something to me.

"Say it again," he whispers in uncertainty, wearing a look that I can only assume is shock and admiration.

"I love you, Jackson. I know I've never said it, and I'm sorry. But, baby, I don't want to live another fucking moment without you knowing how much you mean to me." Before I can get another word out, he presses his lips to mine in a soft, claiming kiss, then he pulls back. His eyes dart between mine, and the corner of his mouth tilts into a half smile.

"I have been in love with you since we were kids,

baby. You know that I love you. You are everything to me."

"You already know that I love you." This comes from a groggy Kale, and we both chuckle because he's never held back where his feelings are concerned. Kale has always worn his heart on his sleeve, and I've lost count of how many times I wish I were more like my brother.

Our father wasn't good to us, and with his controlling and abusive tendencies, I didn't want him to send Jackson away. If he knew the truth of our relationship, taking Jax away from us is the first thing our father would have done, and Kale and I wouldn't have survived it.

We'd have never seen Jackson again, and who knows what would have happened to him? We would have been forced to live our lives without him, and that would have been our punishment for being in love.

We might have had money, a good house, and a good education, but our home was still fucking broken.

We didn't have love.

Not until Jackson and Savy.

I know that I'm selfish, but I couldn't risk losing Jackson. And I know that he understood, but it doesn't matter. It doesn't stop the guilt I feel for holding back with him all these years.

There's only one thing missing in my life now, and I'll spend every fucking second I have left on this miserable planet proving to Savannah that we are worth it. I'll show her that, while our love might be messy and unique, it's fucking real, and it's hers if she wants it.

Savannah Carter is ours, and we are hers, and we won't ever let her go.

Guilt.

That's all I felt as they placed my stepfather's coffin into the Jagger family crypt, sealing him behind stone forever. My mother is completely broken, and I don't think she'll ever recover from this.

Kale and Reign stand off to the side, accepting condolences from their father's business associates, while Jackson stands beside my mom, offering her the support that she needs as she says her final good-byes to her husband.

I did this.

I selfishly made last week's dinner about myself, and even though I won't miss my stepfather, it doesn't change the facts.

He's dead because of me.

I haven't spoken more than a sentence to the guys since that night, and it's eating me up inside. I didn't realize they would play such an important role in my happiness, even before the masks. Now that their father is gone, I won't blame them if they never forgive me.

I wanted the men behind the masks to be them so fucking bad that I didn't stop to think about what things would be like if it were actually true. When I saw Kale's mask, I felt like I had been stripped and laid bare, and I wasn't at all prepared for it. I felt everything all at once, and I couldn't shake the part of me that thought that by learning their true identities, I'd have to choose between Jackson and my stepbrother's, or the men behind the masks, and I didn't want to lose either.

That's why it hurt.

Because I had fallen in love with all of them, and I jumped to conclusions as I always do, panicking because I thought I'd lose them forever.

"Savannah, honey, it's time to go." My mother's voice startles me, and I turn to face her. "We're all headed back to the house for Kalvin's wake, would you like to ride with us?" My eyes flick to my grandparents, waiting for us in their car, but the last place I want to be right now is the house where this whole mess started. I don't deserve to celebrate the life of the man whose death is on my hands.

"Mom. I'm so sorry."

"Oh, Savannah!" She pulls me into a warm hug, then draws back to look into my eyes. "Kalvin's accident wasn't your fault, honey. Accidents happen to people every day, and unfortunately, that's just a part of life. We may not have ended on the best of terms, but nothing about what happened was your fault. Please, find it within your heart to let that go, because life is way too short, Savannah. Jackson explained everything to me in a way that I'd understand, and I get it, honey, I really do. You deserve happiness no matter what that looks like for you, and I am not going to stand in your way. You are my daughter and I love you, no matter what."

I stare at my mom, utterly perplexed. I thought she'd be against all this. I thought she'd tell me how wrong it is to be in love with her stepsons and their best friend, and blame me for ruining her family.

Well, I guess they aren't her anything anymore.

I gnaw on my lip, debating her request to head back to the house. Movement catches my eye, and I flick my gaze over Mom's shoulder to see Kale, Reign, and Jackson all enter the crypt where their father now lies. The only way we can all move forward is to see where the four of us stand, which means that I need to talk to them. I can't keep freezing them out, because the elephant in the room isn't getting any smaller.

"Is it okay if I meet you back there?" I search her eyes for signs of her disapproval, but instead, a small smile touches the corner of her lips.

"I think that would be best. They need you more than ever, honey."

"Thanks, Momma." God, I don't deserve this woman. How she can be so understanding in all of this is beyond me. I don't deserve those guys after what I did, either, but I'll be fucking damned if I don't live the rest of my life earning the right to call them mine each day.

I wait for everyone to leave before heading toward the crypt, my nerves going haywire. I feel like I could throw up what little food I have in my stomach at any moment with how nervous I am. Still, I push it down because I have to do this.

As I reach the entrance, I close my eyes and exhale one last steadying breath before putting one foot in front of the other and crossing the threshold. The second my eyes register what's in front of me, I freeze. All three of *my* guys stand there in their masks!

I open my mouth, but no words come out. I'm speechless and confused. Why are they wearing the masks?

"You fell in love with us when you had no idea who we were." Even with his mask on, I can tell that it's Jackson from the clothes he is wearing. His perfectly tailored suit clings to his muscles, and fuck, it does something to me.

"You saw us, the real us, as we hid behind the masks," Reign says, his voice low, as if each word he says to me is a piece of his heart.

Kale steps forward until he is standing directly in front of me. I shiver in anticipation as he slowly reaches out and cups my cheek. "Now that you've seen who we are beneath it all, I wouldn't blame you for walking away. But we have to try, baby girl. We have to let you know just how much you mean to us. But if wearing a mask is the only way I get to keep you, the only way *we* get to keep you, then so fucking be it, because we won't let you go, Savannah. I won't let any cunt take you from me, not even that piece of shit ex of yours."

My eyes widen at Kale's tone, and a thought tugs at the back of my mind, telling me that Blake's disappearance wasn't random.

"He isn't really missing, is he?" I breathe out, and Kale's honey colored eyes darken behind his mask.

"That stupid cunt signed his death warrant the moment he put his hands on what belongs to us, baby girl, and I have no fucking regrets." He speaks with such conviction, and it only drowns out the possibility that he might be lying. "If I recall, you enjoyed watching and partaking in my punishment at the beach that night. Do you remember, baby?"

I gasp. "When you lit the bonfire and I rode both their cocks? Of course I remember." They all laugh at my words before Kale clears his throat to continue.

"How does it feel to know that your ex was lying lifeless at the bottom of that cliff while we fucked you?"

I'm sick in the head.

I'm so fucking twisted because I don't even feel any remorse. Hell, I'm not even shocked that he's fucking dead. That asshole was bound to have it coming someday. The way he treated women was alarming, and he was on a one-way ticket to turning into my stepfather.

My pussy throbs at the thought of them claiming me while Blake's dead body was nearby, and I shouldn't be so turned on, but I am.

These fucking guys drive me crazy.

They push my boundaries in a way that awakens something dark in me, that nobody will ever understand. Who the fuck am I to say no to this, when I want whatever this is between us more than anything?

I reach and push Kale's mask up, resting it on the top of his head. The sight of his handsome face has me smiling, because seeing him like this, all dressed up and staring down at me like he loves me, makes me never want to risk losing them again.

Before I met the masked version of them, I didn't think I'd ever get the chance to love them the way I had always wanted to. But now that they are standing before me, their hearts on their sleeves, I realize that I was never alone in this, even when I felt like I was.

I can't let them go.

"If I choose this... Do I get to have all three of you? Because I don't think I could ever choose. I am in love with you all. Kale, Reign, and Jackson. You have my heart. I've never loved anyone else." My stomach sinks when they take a while to answer, and panic sears through my chest at the possibility of having to choose, but when Reign and Jackson both remove their masks and come to stand on either side of Kale, the panic slowly eases.

"We're a package deal, Little Viper. If you want one of us, then you have to take all of us," Reign growls, sending a delicious shiver down my spine.

"We've been obsessed with you for years. You had us hanging on your every word like a bunch of lovesick fools, begging for a shred of your attention. We loved you then, we love you now, and we'll love you till we're a pile of fucking bones in a box inside this crypt. You have us, Savannah. And there is no way out," Jax declares, causing the other two to nod their agreement. Kale and Reign take one of Jackson's hands, holding it in their own. They are reaching for comfort in a moment shadowed by uncertainty, and I decide to put them out of their misery.

"I want this," I blurt out. "Almost my whole fucking life, I've wanted this with you. All of you. Please. I know that I fucked up with your dad, but I promise I'll spend the rest of my life trying to make it up to you."

"Savy, baby, stop. No," Reign's voice breaks over my raging thoughts, and my eyes stare up into his dark ones. "Savy, you beautiful woman. That man does not matter to us. The accident had nothing to do with any of us. Shit happens, Savy. He will not be missed by us, that much is true. Please, Little Viper, believe me when I tell you that I would have walked out on him years ago if I could have taken you with me," he says, his voice raw, but still comforting.

"Me too, Savannah," Kale adds.

"You already know it, baby girl," Jackson says, and my heart is beating so fast behind my rib bones that I think I am having a fucking heart attack at how full it feels.

All three of them grin when they realize from my expression that I am all in, then they each exchange a glance before focusing back on me. I swallow audibly as they pull on their masks and step back, leaving me feeling cold without their warmth.

"Ready or not, Little Viper," Kale says in a seductive tone.

"What?" I ask.

"You have thirty seconds to run or we'll fuck you right here as a final goodbye to our father," Reign says, reaching behind him to grab the chain hanging on the wall. My jaw unhinges, and my pussy pulses with pure, unadulterated need at the thought of them chaining me to this crypt and fucking me senseless before their freshly buried father.

I know I shouldn't, but after the years of abuse he has forced the twins and my mom to suffer through, I can't help but think that maybe my guys need to do this for them. To settle whatever score they have with their father, that will never be settled now that he's dead. Besides, this can be our dirty little secret.

I reach up and push the straps of my dress down my arms and let it fall to the ground, loving the way all three of their gazes darken at the sight of me in my strapless bra and black lacy panties. I stretch my arms out before me, palms facing upward, ready for their chains.

"Chain me. I want you to chain me to this crypt and fuck me till I'm screaming your names loud enough to wake the dead. Let's send that mother-fucker to hell with a bang." They are the devils I know, and I would gladly burn for all eternity if it means I get to feel their cocks moving inside every one of my holes each day.

I will always belong to them—Kale, Reign, and Jackson—and they will always belong to me.

Together forever, with no exit.

A vow that only we understand.

There is no salvation in a bond like ours, and we don't want to be fucking saved.

Because the dirtier the secret, the sweeter the sin.

I bet you want to be chased by three masked men in the woods now, huh?

Thank you so much for reading Dirty Little Secret. We seriously loved writing Savannah, Kale, Reign, and Jackson's story. The fact that they were twins made it so much more fun! These novellas have been so fucking fun to write, and we cannot wait to jump into the next one.

Want to know where River was the night Kalvin died? Or should we say, who was driving the other car? Keep an eye out for the pre-order for book 2.

STALKER LINKS

Newsletter 
Facebook 
Reader's Group 
Instagram 
TikTok 
Amazon 
Website 
Bookbub ♡
Goodreads ♡
Linktree ♡

Octavia's 'Tainted Hearts Society' is where you'll see it all first!

This is a space created for Octavia to connect with her readers, talk about her characters, and announce upcoming projects, bookish news, artwork, and any information and exclusive sneak peeks that she has not yet shared with the world.

Join my Newsletter!

TIKTOK 🤍

INSTAGRAM🤍

FACEBOOK🤍

AUTHOR PAGE 🤍

WEBSITE🤍

GOODREADS🤍

LINKTREE 🤍

Also By Samantha Barrett

Mafia Romance's

https://books.bookfunnel.com/mafiaseries

Secret Society/ Bully/ Masked Men

https://books.bookfunnel.com/dirtytemptation

Sinners Welcome (Pure Smut Novellas)

https://books.bookfunnel.com/sinnerswelcome

Samantha's Entire Backlist

https://books.bookfunnel.com/SamanthasBookverse

Wreck and Ruin

Forevermore Book One

A dark, gothic little mermaid retelling.

https://mybook.to/wreckandruin

View Octavia's Website for the Full list of Content Warnings

WEBSITE: www.octaviaknightly.com

ACKNOWLEDGMENTS

Samantha

Marcus, the man who I get to chase through the woods and play with like my own personal fuck doll. Thank you for always being so good about role playing and letting me put anything inside you for research purposes, you the real motherfucking MVP my man!

My children, you may never be able to look Octavia in the eye again if you ever read this book but, at least you know mommy isn't the only one who is fucked up, haha.

My mummy, my queen, my life giver, thank you for always loving me and being there whenever I needed you, you are my world. I love you beyond measure.

Dad, my king, my best friend, my rock, I love you old man more than you will ever know.

Octavia, you are a fucking queen! Thank you for making this so fun and going on this wild ride with me. I love you my bestie from another testie. I am so grateful for your friendship and trust in me to write one of these smutty little books, you filthy girl you were a pro at this shit.

Sarah, I have no words to describe how much you mean to me, you are the backbone to this whole thing and without you I wouldn't be where I am. I love you babe.

My alpha's, Debbie, Clare, Erin and Samantha (number 2), you nasty bitches mean the fucking world to me and I love that you trust me with every book to give you the HEA you are all craving. Thank you for being the best hype team ever!

My beta babes, Amber, Amanda, Nicole, Patti, Morgan, Alex & Rizzo, we can't thank you enough for beta reading this book and loving these characters as much as we do. You ladies have helped us more than you know.

My ARC army girls, you dirty bitches are coming to hell with me! You know it and so do I, I'm kidding. Thank you ladies for being here and loving these books the way you do it means the fucking world to me.

Lizz, you are way too good to me and I can never repay you for the amount of time and effort you put into these books. You are a fucking angel and I love you dearly.

My darling dark, delicious readers, thank you again for following me and reading each of these books. I cannot tell you how much it means to me that you follow me on this ride and love each of these characters as much as I do.

Sam xxx

ACKNOWLEDGMENTS

Octavia

Scotty, thank you for being the most incredible father to our children I could have ever asked for. Thank you for your unwavering support and endless words of encouragement in making my dreams of becoming an author a reality. For putting up with my deranged ideas, which just keep getting more depraved the longer I am in this gig. For all that you are, all that you do, and for everything else in between. My mainframe, my guiding light in the dark, I love you forevermore. Always have, always will.

Mumma, the woman who gave me my life's blood. You are the strongest woman I know, and I am proud to call you my best friend. Thank you for sharing with me your passion for literature. And even more so, thank you for sharing the writing gene with me. Without you, I am nothing. My therapist. My lifeline. I will not apologize for the hundred and one phone calls a day. I love you more than air. PS. I like the high ones. PPS. *This one is dirty.*

Sammy, my girl, my kindred spirit, my cheerleader. Babe, what can I say? Years of friendship, and we are finally co-writing together. Wouldn't be able to do it without you, babe. *"You are absolutely feral, but I love you for it."* From the bottom of my black heart, I love you.

Kristy, my love. You have been my rock for years now, and I would be lost without you. Your words of encouragement and wisdom are what keep me going when impostor syndrome shows its ugly head. I'm incredibly honored to call you my friend. Thank you for your guidance and for believing in me. I love you to your bones!

Aaden James, if you are reading over my shoulder, I'd probably give this one a miss. It's just smut. Miss you every day. More than all the stars, xo

My dearest Nanna. I lost you this year. To say it has been hard is a severe understatement. Thank you for being proud of me. Thank you for all your love. I wish you were here. P.S. You would have liked this one, Nan. *It's filthy.*

Thank you to my alpha readers, Erin, Debbie, Samantha W, Lynn, and Sarah. Your help and support were absolutely needed whilst on this wild journey. This one's even dirtier. I will forever be grateful to you guys. Thank you, xo

To our Beta girlies, your commentary was everything we needed to help make Kale, Reign, and Jackson's story come to life. Thank you, xo

To my Street Team, thank you for being so wonderful. I am so grateful to all. None of this would be possible without you.

Sarah, my PA, my right-hand man, my friend. Without you, I wouldn't be here, girl. You have supported me through it all, and there are no words I could use that would ever express how grateful I am for you. I love you, and I mean it!

And last but not least, thank *you*, my Tainted little readers. The fact that you're reading my books means everything to me. Thank you for loving my characters as much as I love writing them, and for sticking by me on this wild, wild ride. I am grateful to all of you.

From the bottom of my Tainted heart, thank you.

Octavia xx

Samantha Barrett is originally from Auckland, New Zealand but living in Brisbane, Australia.

Sam writes all things dirty dark and delicious with a side of twisted mind fuck.

She is a lover of all things red flags and an anti-hero is a must.

Octavia Knightly is a Modern Gothic and Dark Romance Author from a cozy forest town on the East Coast of Australia. When she's not writing, reading, or listening to music, you'll find her picking flowers and surviving on coffee. She's either planning her next heartbreaking story or something dark, dirty, and depraved. Obsessed with the color morally black, Octavia lives for anti-heroes, and worry not, you'll always get your HEA!

Want to know more about Octavia? Follow her on social media, and sign up for her newsletter for exclusive sneak peeks and teasers of her upcoming books!